■SCHOLASTIC

My First Phonics
Jumbo Workbook

This book belongs to:

_____

Editor: Michelle Sturm
Cover design: Tannaz Fassihi
Cover art: Gabriele Antonini
Interior design: Westchester Education Services
Interior illustrations: Westchester Education Services
All other images © Shutterstock.com
ISBN 978-1-338-87392-4

Scholastic Inc., 557 Broadway, New York, NY 10012
Copyright © 2023 Scholastic Inc.
All rights reserved. Printed in the U.S.A.
First printing, January 2023

1 2 3 4 5 6 7 8 9 10   144   32 31 30 29 28 27 26 25 24 23

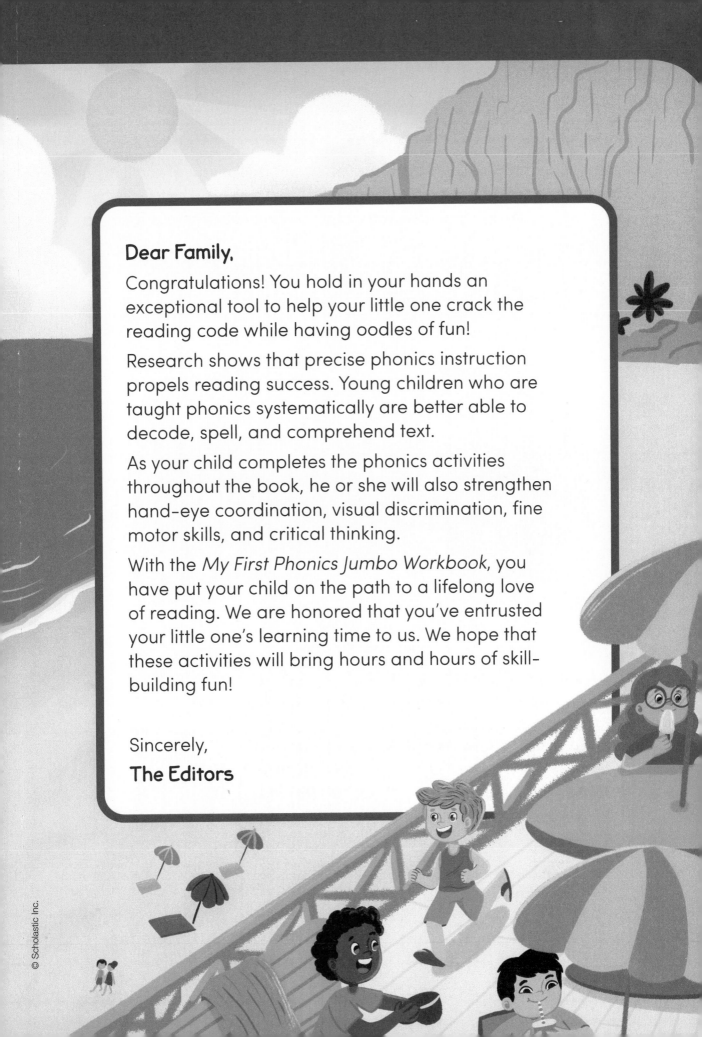

Dear Family,

Congratulations! You hold in your hands an exceptional tool to help your little one crack the reading code while having oodles of fun!

Research shows that precise phonics instruction propels reading success. Young children who are taught phonics systematically are better able to decode, spell, and comprehend text.

As your child completes the phonics activities throughout the book, he or she will also strengthen hand-eye coordination, visual discrimination, fine motor skills, and critical thinking.

With the *My First Phonics Jumbo Workbook*, you have put your child on the path to a lifelong love of reading. We are honored that you've entrusted your little one's learning time to us. We hope that these activities will bring hours and hours of skill-building fun!

Sincerely,

The Editors

About This Book

Your child is ready to embark on the exciting journey of reading! The path to success is a strong phonics foundation. That's why we designed over 250 age-perfect activities and mini-books that walk your child through each sound. Your budding bookworm will enjoy a sequence of playful pages to ensure engagement and learning. Here are some examples:

The goal of this workbook is to teach phonics. But, along the way, children will boost other essential skills, including:

- **Following Directions**
- **Speaking**
- **Reading**
- **Writing**
- **Coloring**

- **Sorting**
- **Cutting***
- **Pasting**
- **Fine Motor**
- **Critical Thinking**

* Always supervise children when working with scissors.

Extra, Extra!

There's more! These special components are guaranteed to make learning extra fun.

PHONICS MINI-BOOKS

This book includes 35 adorable phonics mini-books to teach every letter sound and eight of the most common word families! Simply cut where indicated and fold or staple together. The result? Your child's first learning library!

BRAIN BOOSTERS

Ready for more phonics fun? Check out page 10 for real-world games and activities to deepen your child's phonics understanding.

INSTANT FLASH CARDS

Snip out the flash cards for letter sounds, sight words, and word families on pages 303–314. For added fun, check out the list of ways to use the cards for instant games.

MOTIVATING STICKERS

What better way to mark the milestones of your child's learning than with colorful stickers? After a workbook session, they're the perfect way to say, "Job well done!"

REWARD CERTIFICATE

Celebrate your child's leap in phonics mastery with this bright, pull-out certificate (page 320).

ONLINE LEARNING GAMES

Take learning online with fun learning games: **www.scholastic.com/success**

Table of Contents

Tips for Success! 8
Read with Your Child 9
Brain Boosters 10

FINE MOTOR SKILLS 11
Left-to-right progression 12
Right-to-left progression 13
Top-to-bottom progression 14
Bottom-to-top progression 15
Diagonal: left-to-right progression 16
Diagonal: right-to-left progression 17
Backward circles 18
Forward circles 19
Arcs 20
Wavy lines 21
Drawing 22

VISUAL DISCRIMINATION SKILLS ... 23
Same and different 24–25
Patterns 26–27
Categorize 28–29
Matching 30
Opposites 31
Spot the difference 32
Hidden picture 33

ALPHABET AND PHONICS 34
Vowel *Aa* 35–40
Consonant *Bb* 41–46
Consonant *Cc* 47–52
Review: *Aa, Bb, Cc* 53–54
Rhyme 55–56
Sight words 57–58

Consonant *Dd* 59–64
Vowel *Ee* 65–70

Consonant *Ff* 71–76
Review: *Dd, Ee, Ff* 77–78
Rhyme 79–80
Sight words 81–82

Consonant *Gg* 83–88
Consonant *Hh* 89–94
Vowel *Ii* 95–100
Review: *Gg, Hh, Ii* 101–102
Rhyme 103–104
Sight words 105–106

Consonant *Jj* 107–112
Consonant *Kk* 113–118
Consonant *Ll* 119–124
Review: *Jj, Kk, Ll* 125–126
Rhyme 127–128
Sight words 129–130

Consonant *Mm* 131–136
Consonant *Nn* 137–142
Vowel *Oo* 143–148
Review: *Mm, Nn, Oo* 149–150
Rhyme 151–152
Sight words 153–154

Consonant *Pp* 155–160
Consonant *Qq* 161–166
Consonant *Rr* 167–172
Review: *Pp, Qq, Rr* 173–174
Rhyme 175–176
Sight words 177–178

Consonant *Ss* 179–184
Consonant *Tt* 185–190
Vowel *Uu* 191–196

My First Phonics Jumbo Workbook

Consonant *Vv* 197–202
Review: *Ss, Tt, Uu, Vv* 203–204
Rhyme 205–206
Sight words 207–208

Consonant *Ww* 209–214
Consonant *Xx* 215–220
Consonant *Yy* 221–226
Consonant *Zz* 227–232
Review: *Ww, Xx, Yy, Zz* 233–234
Rhyme 235–236
Sight words 237–238

Your name 239

WORD FAMILIES 240
Word family **-at** 241–246
Word family **-an** 247–252
Review: **-at** and **-an** 253

Word family **-ip** 255–260
Word family **-ed** 261–266
Review: **-ip** and **-ed** 267

Word family **-en** 269–274
Word family **-ug** 275–280
Review: **-en** and **-ug** 281

Word family **-op** 283–288
Word family **-un** 289–294
Review: **-op** and **-un** 295

Word family review book 297–300

FLASH CARDS 301
Alphabet flash cards 303–308
Word family flash cards 309–310
Sight word flash cards 311–314

Answer key 315–318
Certificate 320

Tips for Success!

Children build essential thinking skills through persistent practice, quality content, and earnest engagement. Here are some quick tips to keep your child's learning time enjoyable, safe, and meaningful.

LEARNING SESSIONS

⭐ **Invite your child to use the workbook a few times a week—or more—whenever you can keep it a joyful experience.** Turn to the pages when your child is alert, focused, and ready to learn. If your child is frustrated or cranky, go to the park or take a book break. We included a list of our favorites on the next page.

⭐ If needed, read the directions aloud, then complete the pages together. As your child grows accustomed to the activities, he or she will likely be able to complete them independently.

SIMPLE SUPPLIES

Nontoxic Crayons: To complete the workbook pages, have a box of crayons easily accessible. Jumbo-sized crayons are great training wheels for children in the early stages of fine-motor progression.

Safety Scissors: The cut-and-paste pages of the workbook require a pair of small safety scissors. **Always supervise children when using scissors.**

Glue: Your child will need a glue stick. A medium- to large-size glue stick is easiest for small hands to grip and manipulate.

Read with Your Child

The world is changing fast, but the act of sitting and reading with a child is timeless. That's why we included **35 mini-books** within the *My First Phonics Jumbo Workbook*! Each colorful, fun book helps bring the focus skill to life. Here are three more ways to support your child's reading:

1. As you read a book, pause to ask your child what might happen next. Read on to confirm or correct your child's prediction.
2. Discuss the characters in the story. Are they kind? Curious? Mischievous? Are they like characters in another book?
3. When you finish a story, have your child retell it.

Here are a few of our very favorite titles.

There Was an Old Lady Who Swallowed the ABCs
by Lucille Colandro

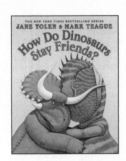

How Do Dinosaurs Stay Friends?
by Jane Yolen and Mark Teague

I Spy Letters
by Jean Marzollo

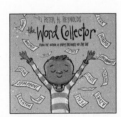

The Word Collector
by Peter H. Reynolds

Is Your Mama a Llama?
by Deborah Guarino

Buzz Said the Bee
by Wendy Cheyette Lewison

Brain Boosters

Make use of these extra activities to support your child's phonics journey. We also encourage you to develop your own creative ideas.

1. **LOOK IN BOOKS:** Choose a secret letter from a page in a picture book. Give your child clues to guess what it is, such as: *It makes the _____ sound. You can hear it at the beginning of _____*. Continue giving clues until your child guesses the letter. Repeat with different letters.

2. **GROCERY STORE TALLY:** Give your child a crayon and a clipboard with a list of five—or more—letters to find at the grocery store. As your child goes through the store with you, challenge him or her to make an X each time a letter is spotted on a product or sign. Which word wins by being spotted the most?

3. **SIGHT WORD COLLAGE:** Choose a single sight word, such as *the,* and encourage your child to cut that word out of magazines—in a variety of sizes and styles. Then use the cuttings to create a colorful sight word collage to display with pride!

4. **MYSTERY BOX:** Place three objects in a box or bag, like a candle, toy car, and carrot for the letter *c.* Encourage your child to name each object and guess the mystery letter at the beginning of each.

5. **FLASH CARD FUN:** On pages 303– 314 you'll find a set of alphabet, sight word, and word family flash cards. Use them with the games on page 302 to expand your young learner's knowledge.

FINE MOTOR SKILLS

Before your little one can write letters, words, and sentences, he or she will need to practice the precise pencil strokes that create them. The pages in this section will help encourage development of fine motor skills. Early mastery of fine motor skills is linked to reading and writing success.

★ Allow your child to first follow the dotted line with a finger, then use a marker, crayon, or pencil to trace.

★ If the straight lines look more like wiggly worms, don't fret. The key is to promote practice and celebrate success.

★ To further reinforce fine motor skills, simply provide blank paper. Encourage your child to draw, scribble, dot, zigzag, and whatever else his or her creativity inspires.

Trace each child's path from left to right.

Trace each animal's path from right to left.

Trace each bird's path down to its nest.

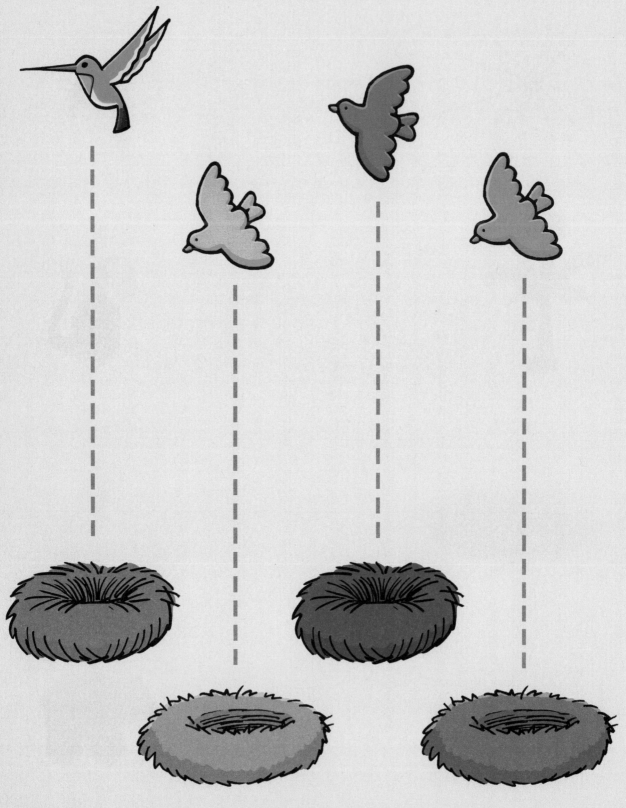

Trace each rocket ship's path up to the planet.

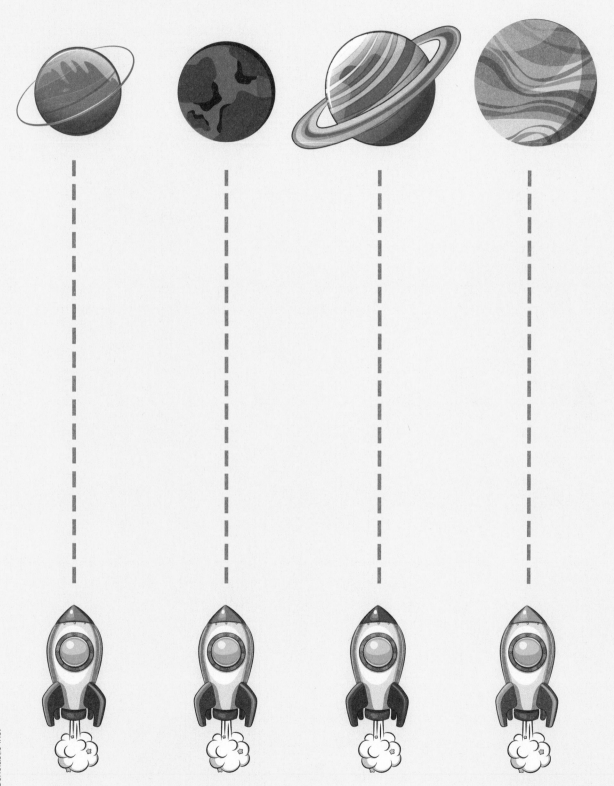

Trace each bee's path up to the beehive.

Trace each ray's path down to the flowers.

Trace each bubble. Start at the dot. Follow the arrow.

Trace each doughnut. Start at the dot. Follow the arrow.

Trace the lines on the rainbow.

Trace each sea creature's path.

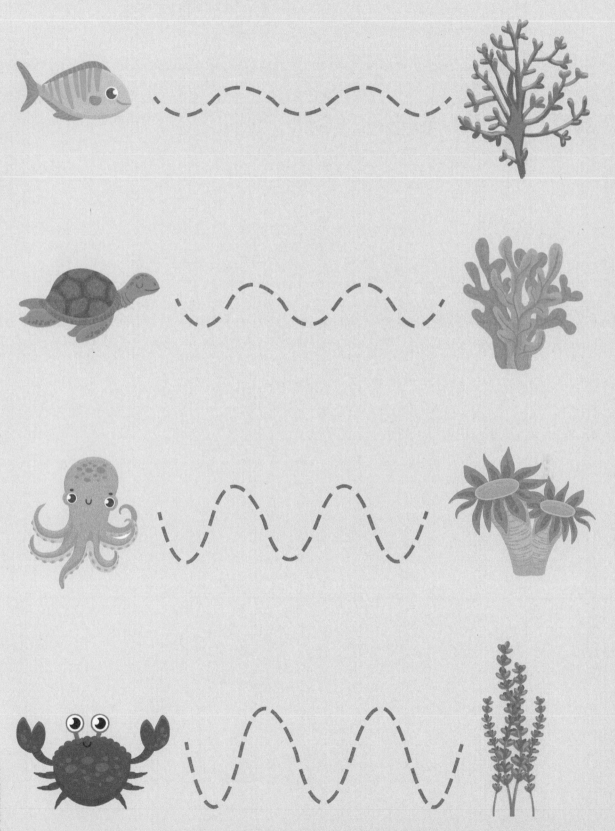

Draw a picture of yourself.

VISUAL DISCRIMINATION SKILLS

Just like fine motor skills, visual discrimination helps build the foundation for reading and writing success. Children can use visual discrimination to detect differences between various objects and shapes. This helps emerging readers to later differentiate between letters, letter combinations, and sounds.

★ Visual discrimination isn't just about the eyes. It's about the brain, too! The eyes team up with the brain to understand and categorize what we see.

★ Play can be purposeful! The following fun, play-based pages help sharpen visual discrimination skills.

★ To further reinforce visual discrimination skills, simply look for groups of objects around you. Encourage your child to separate different types of dried beans, pasta, buttons, blocks, or leaves into categories.

Circle the two pictures on each shelf that are the same.

Color the balloon, dog, and car that is different from the others. Then, color the rest of the picture.

What color comes next?
In each row, color the last picture to continue the pattern.

What shape comes next?
In each row, draw the last shape to continue the pattern.

   _____

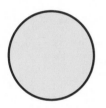    _____

   _____

   _____

Draw a circle around each item you would keep in the bedroom.
Draw a square around each item you would keep in the kitchen.

Write **X** over the object in each row that does not belong.

My First Phonics Jumbo Workbook

Draw a line from each cupcake to its match.

Draw a line from each picture to its opposite.

Find and circle eight differences.

Find and circle the below eight objects in the big picture.

ALPHABET AND PHONICS

Your little one is ready to embark on the exciting journey to reading! Pave your child's path to success with these fun alphabet and phonics activity pages.

★ **ALPHABET**: Encourage your child to recognize each letter in the alphabet and connect it to a particular sound.

★ **RHYMING**: Children learn best by first focusing on the sounds at the beginning of words. However, learning rhyming words allows them to stretch their brains to focus on end sounds, too.

★ **SIGHT WORDS**: Many simple words show up so often that they are best memorized by sight. When young learners have these high-frequency words in their toolboxes, their reading confidence soars.

★ **CUTTING AND PASTING**: Cutting and pasting help build fine motor skills.

Always supervise children when using scissors.

Find and circle seven things that begin with the **a** sound.
The first one has been done for you.

Trace and write **A** and **a**.

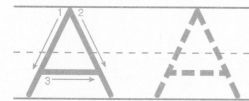

Say the name of each picture.
Write **a** below the picture if it begins with the **a** sound.

Cut out each picture.
If it begins with the **a** sound, paste it on the apple tree.

4

Ants in a cap.

1

Ants!

5

Ants by a can.

8

Ants, ants, ants!

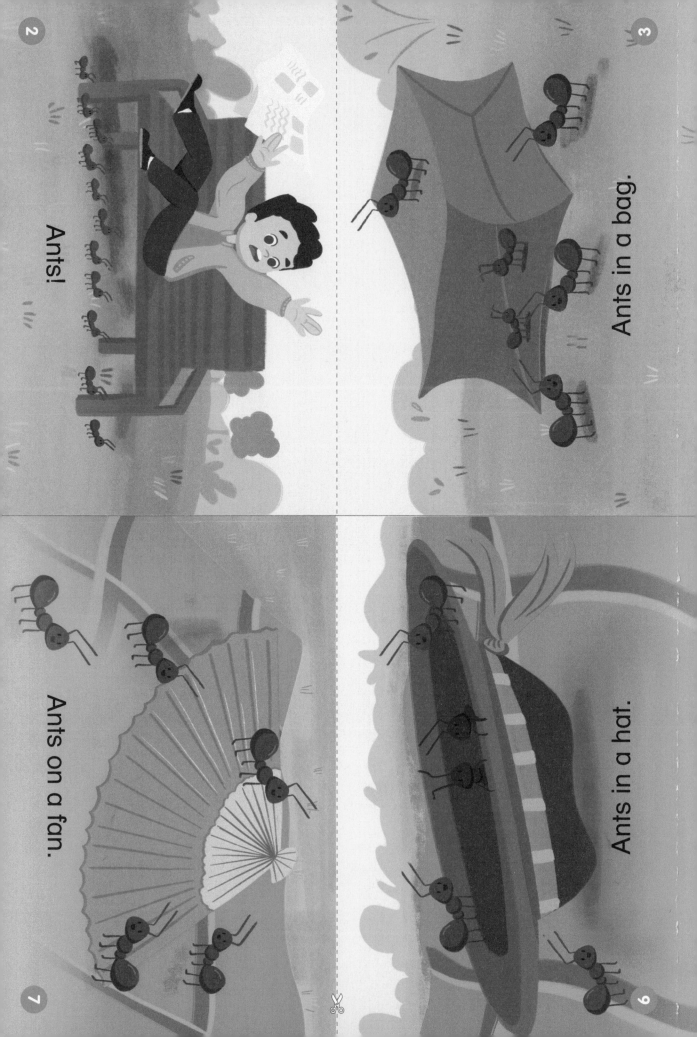

Ants!

Ants in a bag.

Ants in a hat.

Ants on a fan.

Find and circle eight things that begin with the **b** sound.
The first one has been done for you.

Trace and write **B** and **b**.

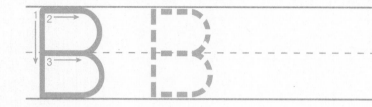

Say the name of each picture. Color it if it begins with the **b** sound. Then, write **b** next to the pictures you colored.

Cut out each picture.
If it begins with the **b** sound, paste it on the beach.

4

Bear rides on a blimp.

Bear's Trip

© Scholastic Inc.

Bear is going to the beach!

1

8

5

Bear rides on a bulldozer.

Bear rides on a bike.

Bear rides on a bus.

Where is bear going?

Bear rides on a boat.

Find and circle seven things that begin with the **c** sound.
The first one has been done for you.

Trace and write **C** and **c**.

Say the name of each picture.
Write **c** next to the picture if it begins with the **c** sound.

Cut out each picture.
If it begins with the **c** sound, paste it on the checkout counter.

4

I can see a cowboy.

I Can See ...

© Scholastic Inc.

1

5

I can see a cat.

I can see a cap.

8

I can see a cow.

I can see a cake.

I can see a car.

I can see a camel.

Draw lines to connect the matching uppercase and lowercase letters. The first one has been done for you.

A —— a	b
c	a
B	C

B	a
c	b
A	C

a	c
b	B
C	A

B	a
A	b
C	c

Say the name of each item.
Write the letter that makes the beginning sound.

_____

- - - - - - - - -

_____

_____

- - - - - - - - -

_____

_____

- - - - - - - - -

_____

_____

- - - - - - - - -

_____

_____

- - - - - - - - -

_____

_____

- - - - - - - - -

_____

Draw a line to connect the pictures that rhyme.
The first one has been done for you.

Color the pictures in each row that rhyme.

Write the missing letter in each box. Use words from the Word List.

Word List
the   can   and   of

th☐   o☐   ☐nd   c☐n

ca☐   t☐e   ☐f   a☐d

Use the words from above to complete the sentences.

I _____ juggle.

I juggle at _____ party.

I juggle apples _____ oranges.

I eat one _____ the oranges.

Sight words: the, of, can, and

Color the picture. Use the Color Key.

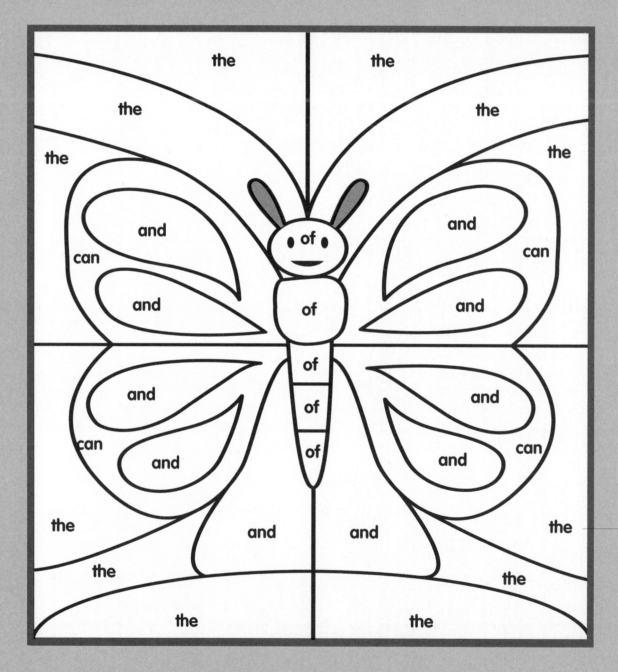

© Scholastic Inc.

Find and circle eight things that begin with the **d** sound.
The first one has been done for you.

Trace and write **D** and **d**.

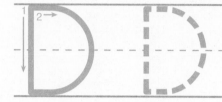

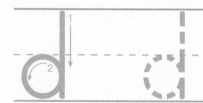

Say the name of each picture. Color it if it begins with the **d** sound. Then, write **d** below the pictures you colored.

Cut out each picture.
If it begins with the **d** sound, paste it on the dance floor.

We like tall dogs.

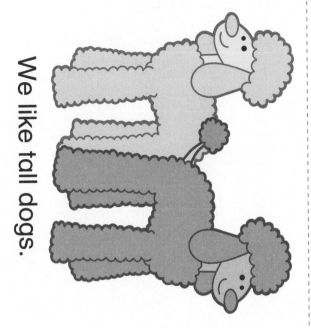

We Like Dogs

We like short dogs.

We like all dogs.

We like big dogs.

We like little dogs.

We like loud dogs.

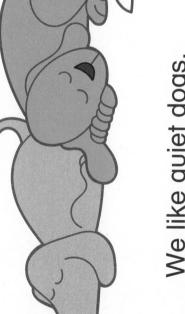

We like quiet dogs.

Find and circle six things that begin with the **e** sound.
The first one has been done for you.

Trace and write **E** and **e**.

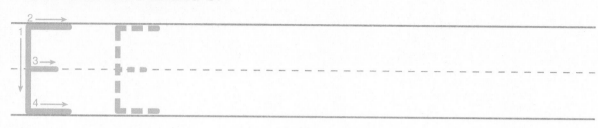

Say the name of each picture.
Write **e** below the picture if it begins with the **e** sound.

Cut out each picture.
If it begins with the **e** sound, paste it on top of the elephant.

Ed likes eggs.

Ed likes eggs at a desk.

Ed likes eggs on a bed.

Ed likes eggs on an engine.

Ed likes eggs.

Ed likes eggs at a desk.

Ed likes eggs on a bed.

Ed likes eggs on an engine.

Find and circle six things that begin with the **f** sound.
The first one has been done for you.

Trace and write **F** and **f**.

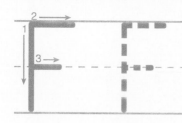

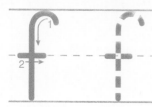

Say the name of each picture. Color it if it begins with the **f** sound. Then, write **f** below the pictures you colored.

Cut out each picture.
If it begins with the **f** sound, paste it on the farm.

I am furry.

I have a big tail.

Four Furry Feet

I am a

_____

I have four feet.

I have big friends.

What am I?

I am red.

Draw lines to connect the matching uppercase and lowercase letters. The first one has been done for you.

F   d

e   f

D   E

D   f

E   e

F   d

E   d

D   F

f   e

e   E

F   f

D   d

Say the name of each picture.
Write the letter that makes the beginning sound.

_ _ _ _ _ _ _ _ _ _

_ _ _ _ _ _ _ _ _ _

_ _ _ _ _ _ _ _ _ _

_ _ _ _ _ _ _ _ _ _

_ _ _ _ _ _ _ _ _ _

_ _ _ _ _ _ _ _ _ _

Draw a line to connect the pictures that rhyme.
The first one has been done for you.

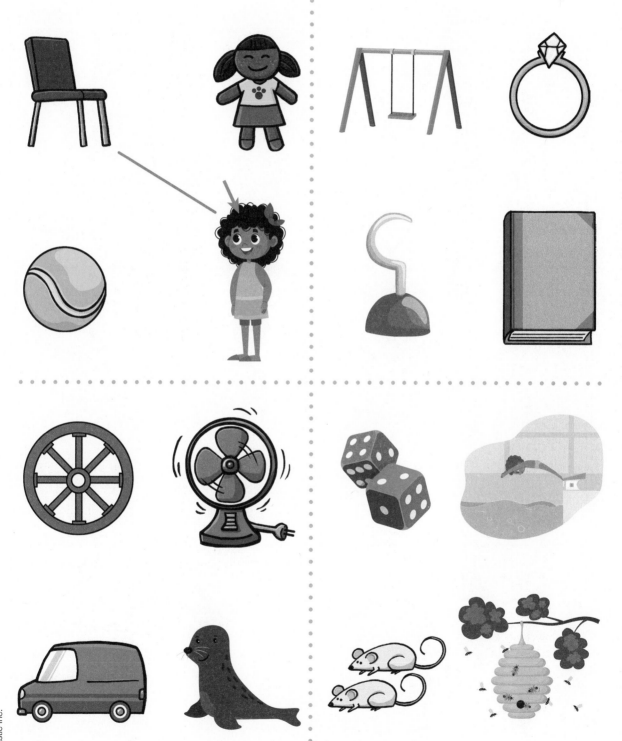

Say the name of each picture. Color the pairs that rhyme.

Write the missing letter in each box. Use words from the Word List.

Word List
to   is   am   you

t ☐   a ☐   ☐ s   yo ☐

i ☐   y ☐ u   ☐ o   ☐ m

Use the words from above to complete the sentences.

We go _____ school.

School _____ fun.

I _____ in Pre-K.

Do _____ go to school?

Color the picture. Use the Color Key.

Color Key

you	is	am	to

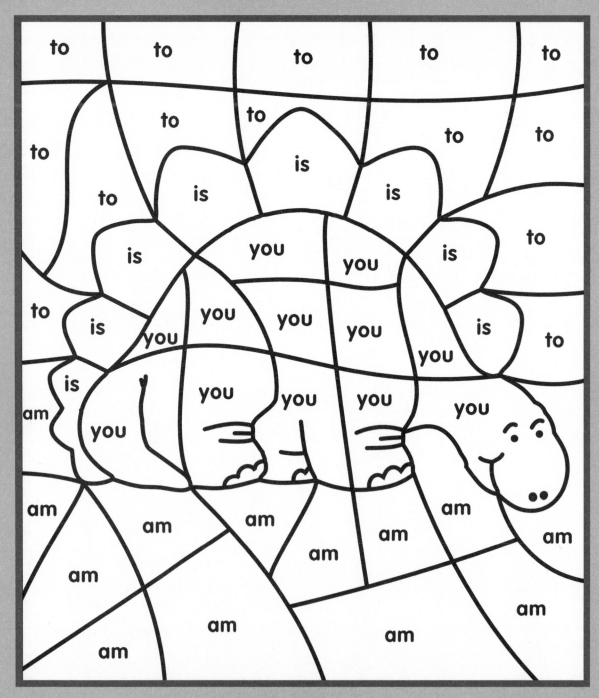

Find and circle seven things that begin with the **g** sound. The first one has been done for you.

Trace and write **G** and **g**.

Say the name of each picture.
Write **g** below the picture if it begins with the **g** sound.

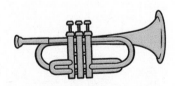

Cut out each picture.
If it begins with the **g** sound, paste it on the game.

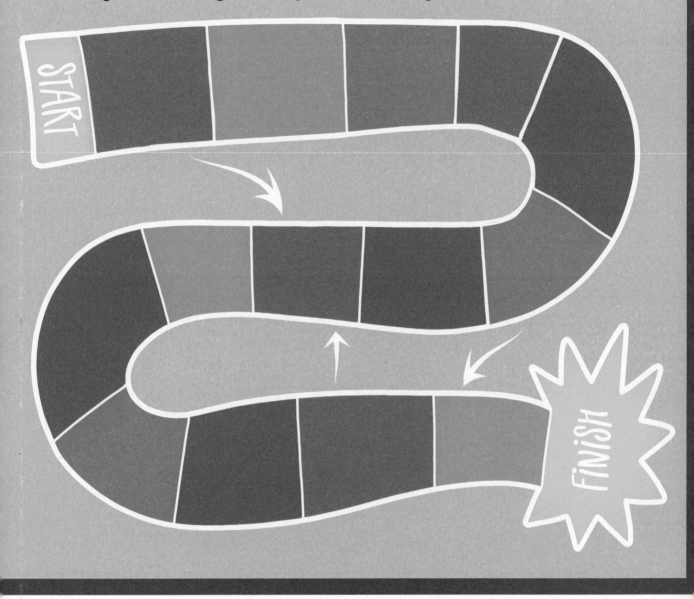

We go by a goat.

Let's Go!

We go by a gate.

Let's go!

GAS STATION

GAS

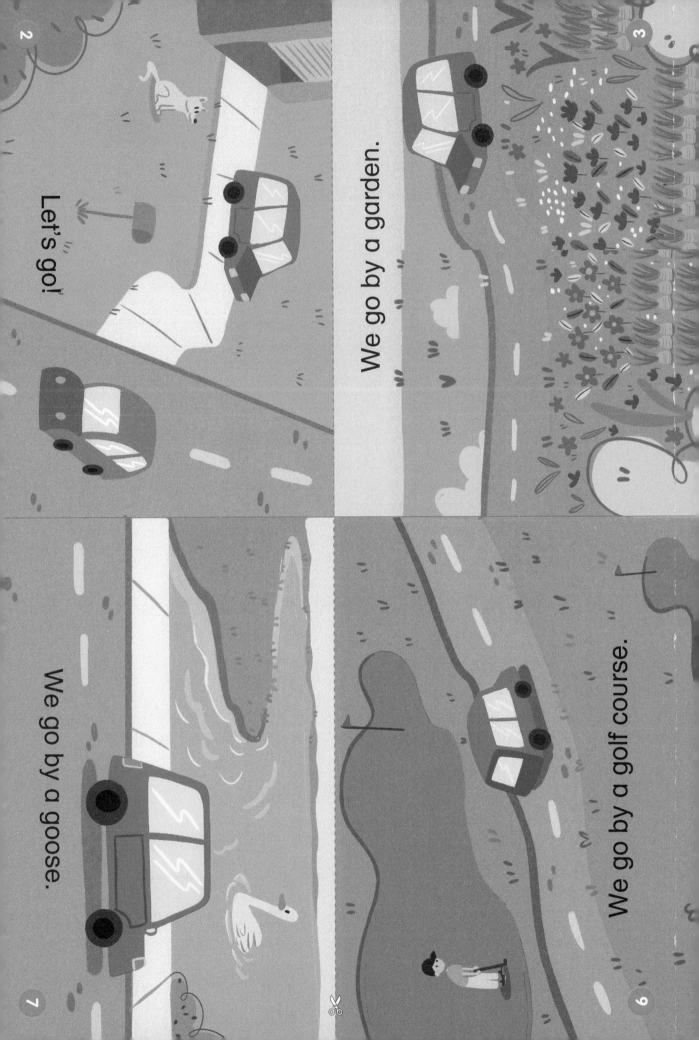

Let's go!

We go by a garden.

We go by a goose.

We go by a golf course.

Find and circle seven things that begin with the **h** sound.
The first one has been done for you.

Trace and write **H** and **h**.

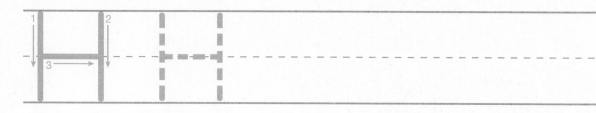

Say the name of each picture. Color it if it begins with the **h** sound. Then, write **h** below the pictures you colored.

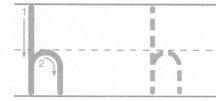

Cut out each picture.
If it begins with the **h** sound, paste
it on the house.

I like my hat.

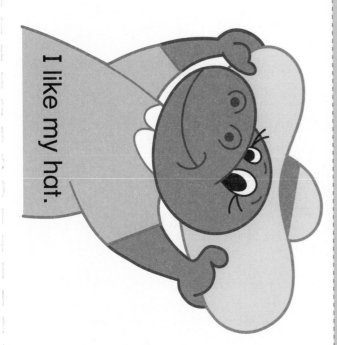

A Happy Hippo

I like my horn.

I am a happy hippo.

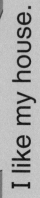

I am a happy hippo.

I like my house.

I like my harp.

I like my honey.

Find and circle six things that begin with the **i** sound.
The first one has been done for you.

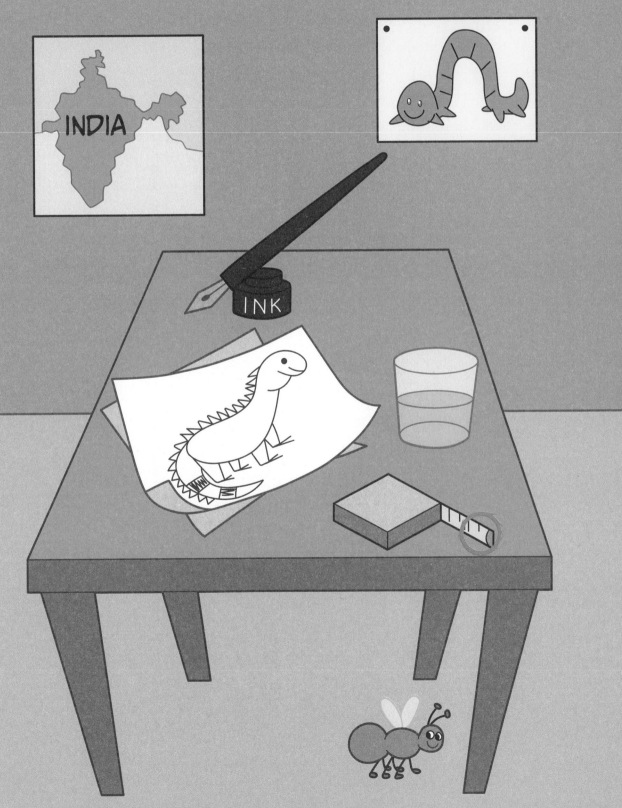

Trace and write **I** and **i**.

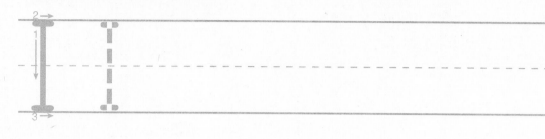

Say the name of each picture. Color it if it begins with the **i** sound.
Then, write **i** below the pictures you colored.

Cut out each picture.
If it begins with the **i** sound, paste it on the invitation.

4

How many inches is I**g**?

How Many Inches?

© Scholastic Inc.

8

How many inches is In**a**?

5

How many inches is I**p**?

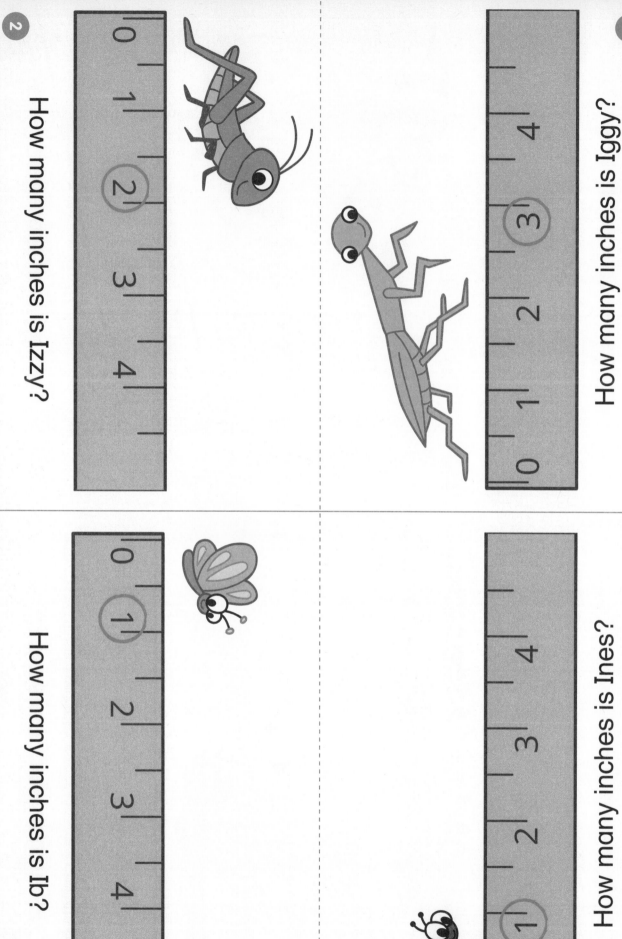

How many inches is Izzy?

How many inches is Iggy?

How many inches is Ines?

How many inches is Ib?

Draw lines to connect the matching uppercase and lowercase letters. The first one has been done for you.

H   G

g   h

I   i

i   h

G   g

H   I

I   i

h   H

g   G

g   I

i   h

H   G

Say the name of each picture.
Write the letter that makes the beginning sound.

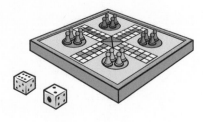

Draw a line to connect the pictures that rhyme.
The first one has been done for you.

Say the name of each picture. Color the pairs that rhyme.

Write the missing letter in each box. Use words from the Word List.

Word List
that   it   he   was

th⬜t   i⬜   ⬜e   wa⬜

w⬜s   t⬜at   ⬜t   ⬜e

Use the words from above to complete the sentences.

Yesterday _____ rained.

Max _____ outside.

Was he in _____ mud?

Did _____ get a bath?

Color the picture. Use the Color Key.

Color Key

he   that   it   was

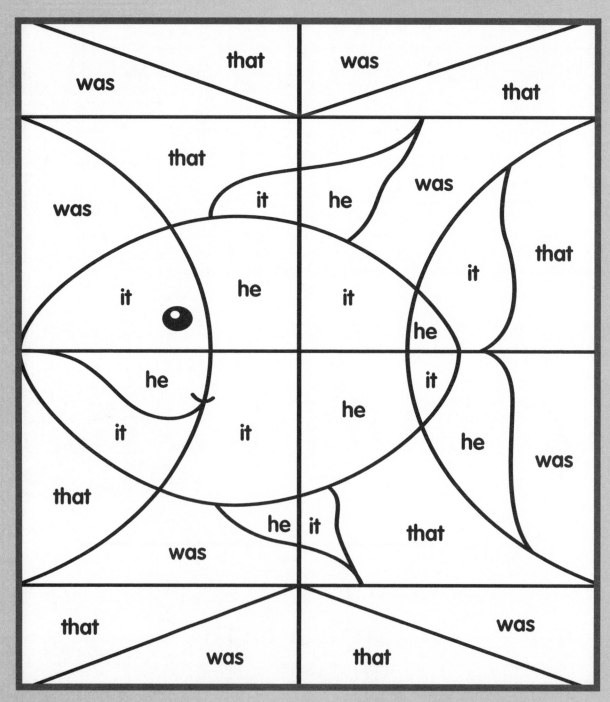

© Scholastic Inc.

Find and circle six things that begin with the **j** sound.
The first one has been done for you.

Trace and write **J** and **j**.

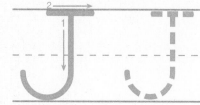

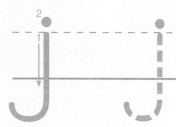

Say the name of each picture. Color it if it begins with the **j** sound. Then, write **j** below the pictures you colored.

Cut out each picture.
If it begins with the **j** sound, paste it on the journal.

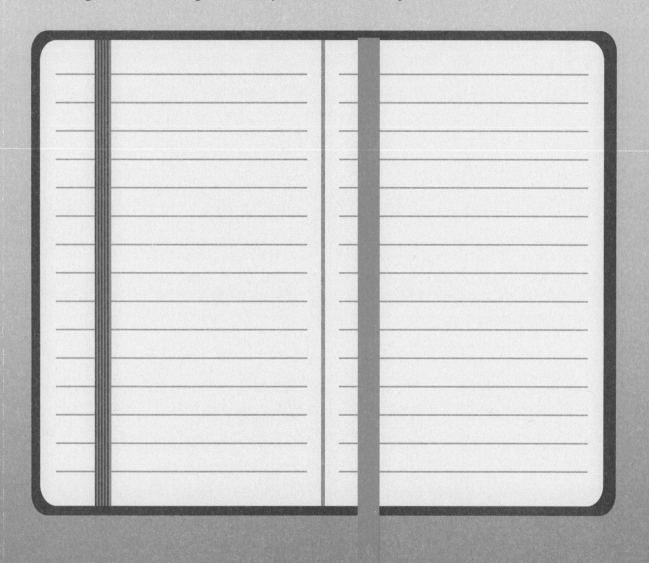

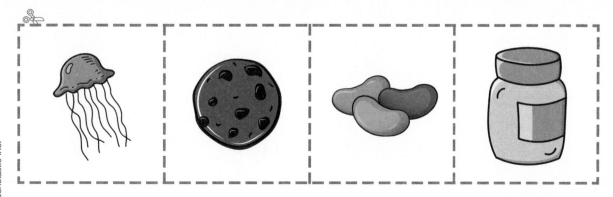

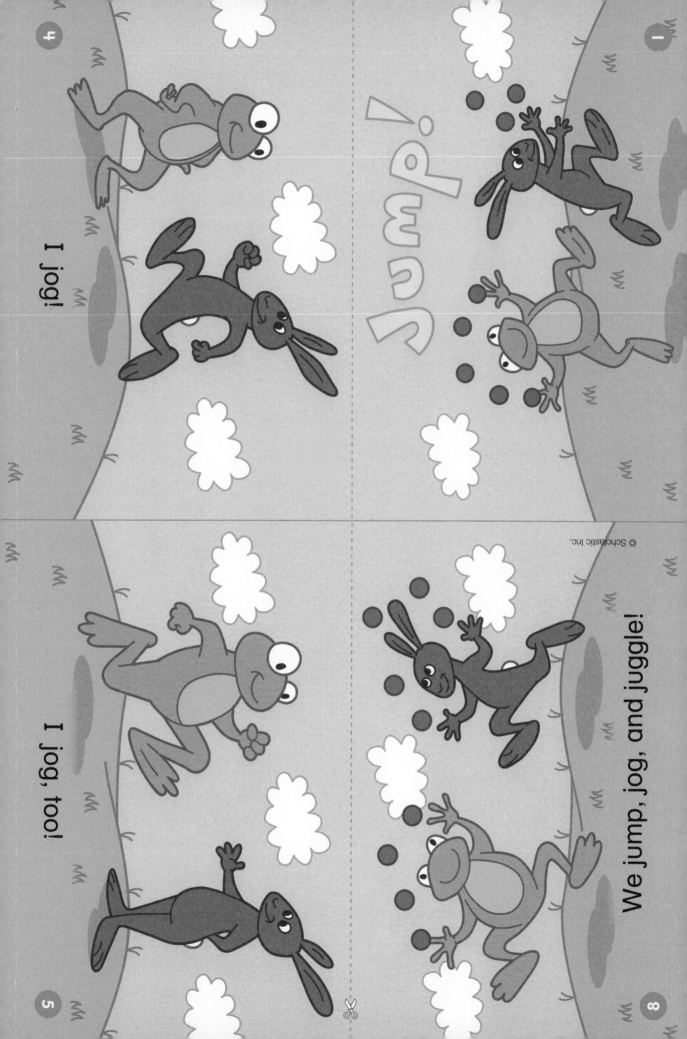

I jog!

Jump!

I jog, too!

We jump, jog, and juggle!

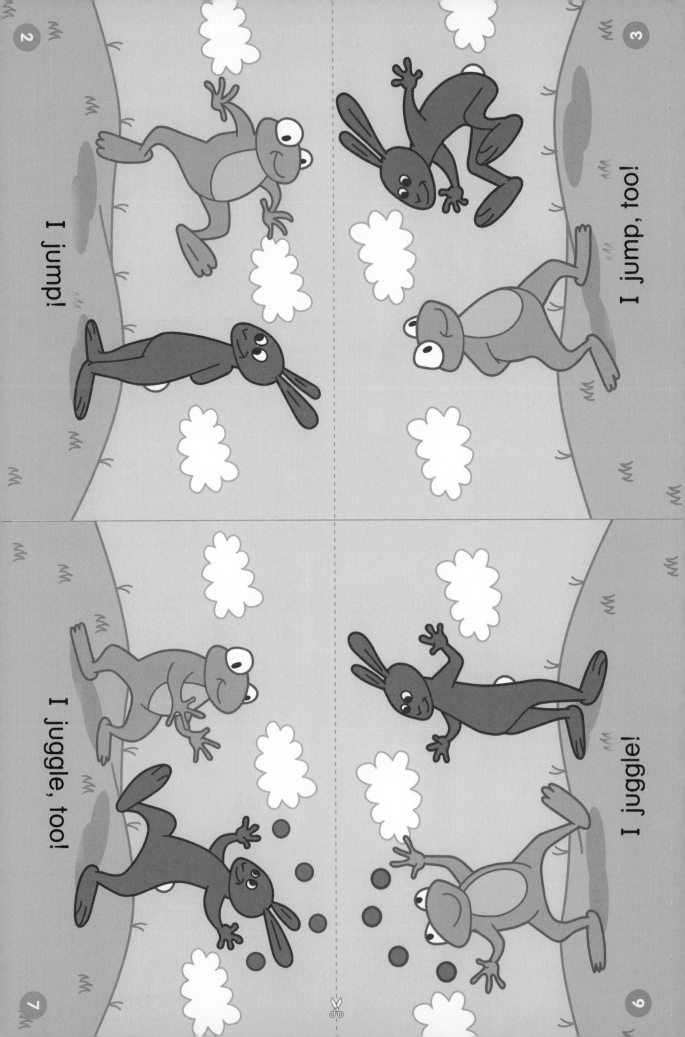

I jump!

I jump, too!

I juggle!

I juggle, too!

Find and circle six things that begin with the **k** sound.
The first one has been done for you.

Trace and write **K** and **k**.

Say the name of each picture.
Write **k** below the picture if it begins with the **k** sound.

Cut out each picture.
If it begins with the **k** sound, paste it on the kite.

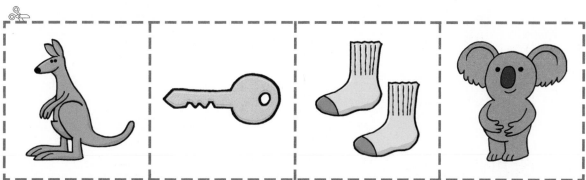

Kevin

Kevin likes koalas.

Kevin likes kangaroos.

I like

Kevin likes kites.

Kevin likes kittens.

What do you like?

Kevin likes ketchup.

Find and circle six things that begin with the **l** sound.
The first one has been done for you.

Trace and write **L** and **l**.

Say the name of each picture. Color it if it begins with the **l** sound.
Then, write **l** below the pictures you colored.

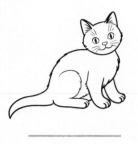

Cut out each picture.
If it begins with the **l** sound, paste it in the lunchbox.

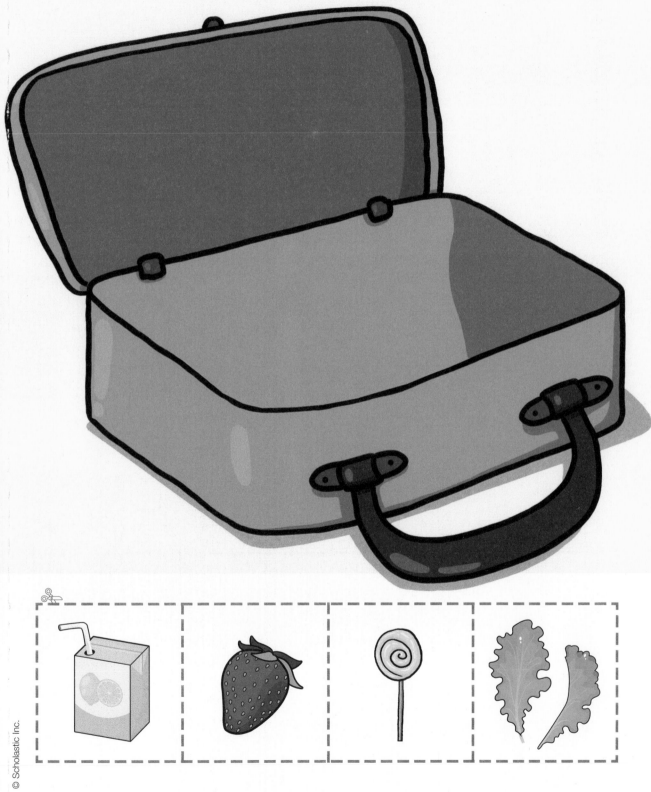

Look! What do you see?

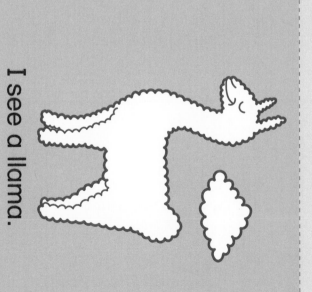

I see a llama.

Look!

What do you see?

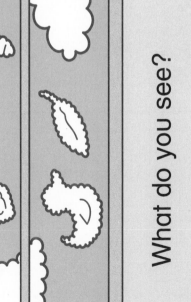

Look! What do you see?

I see a lion.

I see a lamp.

Look! What do you see?

Draw lines to connect the matching uppercase and lowercase letters. The first one has been done for you.

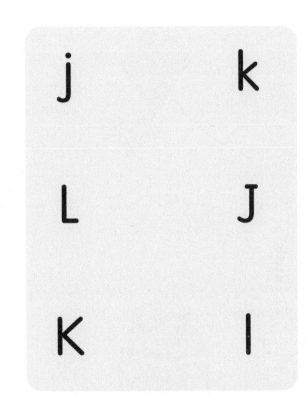

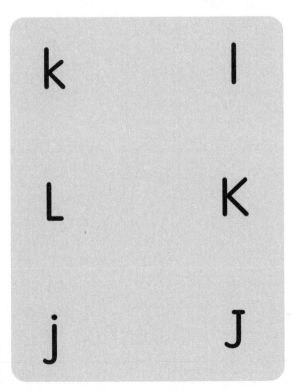

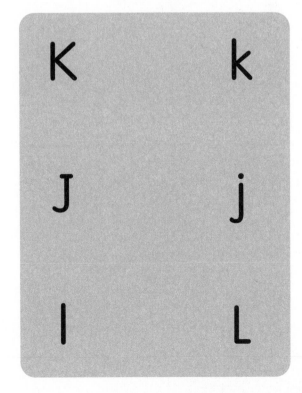

Say the name of each picture.
Write the letter that makes the beginning sound.

_ _ _ _ _ _ _ _ _

_ _ _ _ _ _ _ _ _

_ _ _ _ _ _ _ _ _

_ _ _ _ _ _ _ _ _

_ _ _ _ _ _ _ _ _

_ _ _ _ _ _ _ _ _

_ _ _ _ _ _ _ _ _

_ _ _ _ _ _ _ _ _

_ _ _ _ _ _ _ _ _

_ _ _ _ _ _ _ _ _

_ _ _ _ _ _ _ _ _

_ _ _ _ _ _ _ _ _

Listen to the poem as your parent or caregiver reads it aloud.

> Today I will make my famous mud pie.
> I'll fill it with dirt, leaves, and a fly.
>
> I'll toss in a ring
> I found under my swing.
>
> I'll even add an old dog bone,
> Some twigs, and a stone.
>
> Muddy mud covers the top.
> Uh-oh! Mom's home. Grab a mop!

Draw a line to connect the pictures that rhyme.
The first one has been done for you.

© Scholastic Inc.

Say the name of each picture. Color the pairs that rhyme.

Write the missing letter in each box. Use words from the Word List.

Word List
for   on   are   as

fo ☐   o ☐   ☐re   a ☐

a ☐ e   ☐ s   f ☐ r   ☐ n

Use the words from above to complete the sentences.

We _____ at home.

This one is _____ you.

Put it _____ top.

My sister is as tall _____ me.

Color the picture. Use the Color Key.

Color Key

| for | are | on | as |

Find and circle seven things that begin with the **m** sound.
The first one has been done for you.

Trace and write **M** and **m**.

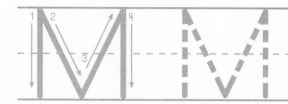

Say the name of each picture.
Write **m** below the picture if it begins with the **m** sound.

Cut out each picture.
If it begins with the **m** sound, paste it on the mountains.

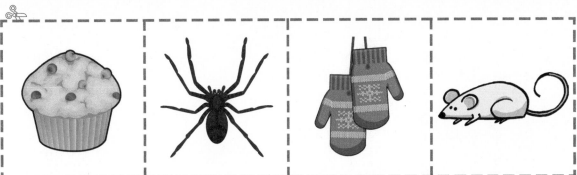

4

Where is the monkey?

1

Where Is the Muffin?

5

Where is the moose?

8

Where is the _____ ?

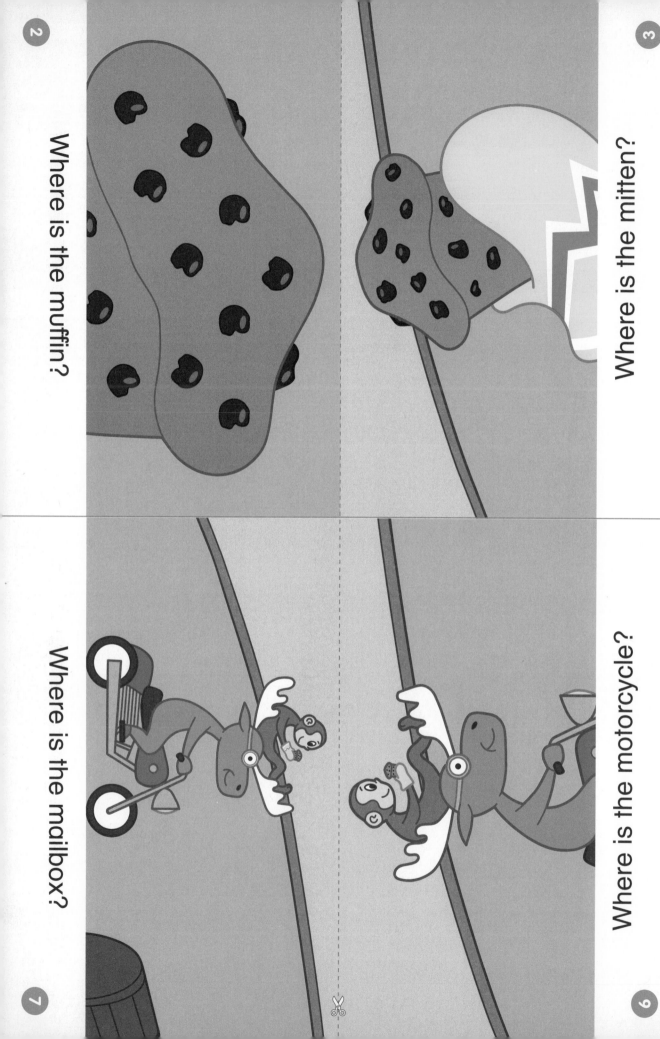

Where is the muffin?

Where is the mitten?

Where is the mailbox?

Where is the motorcycle?

Find and circle six things that begin with the **n** sound.
The first one has been done for you.

Trace and write **N** and **n**.

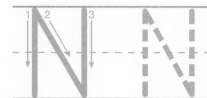

Say the name of each picture. Color it if it begins with the **n** sound. Then, write **n** below the pictures you colored.

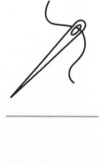

Cut out each picture.
If it begins with the **n** sound, paste it in the net.

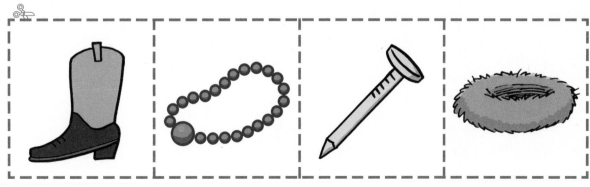

Can you see nine dogs?

Nine

Can you see nine frogs?

Can you draw nine circles?

4

5

8

1

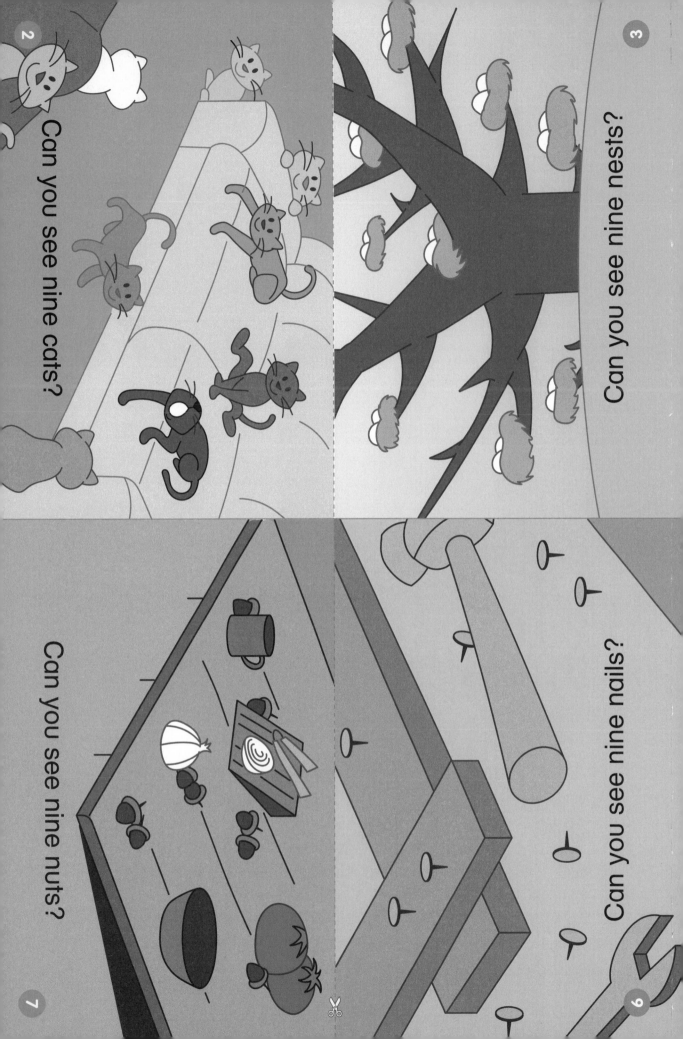

Can you see nine cats?

Can you see nine nests?

Can you see nine nuts?

Can you see nine nails?

Find and circle seven things that begin with the **o** sound.
The first one has been done for you.

Trace and write **O** and **o**.

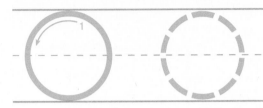

Say the name of each picture. Color it if it begins with the **o** sound. Then, write **o** below the pictures you colored.

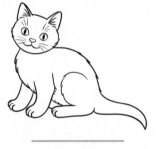

Cut out each picture.
If it begins with the **o** sound, paste it in the office.

4

Ostrich gets on Otter.

Octopus Gets
the Olives

1

© Scholastic Inc.

Octopus gets on Ostrich.

5

Octopus falls on Ostrich, Otter, and Ox!

8

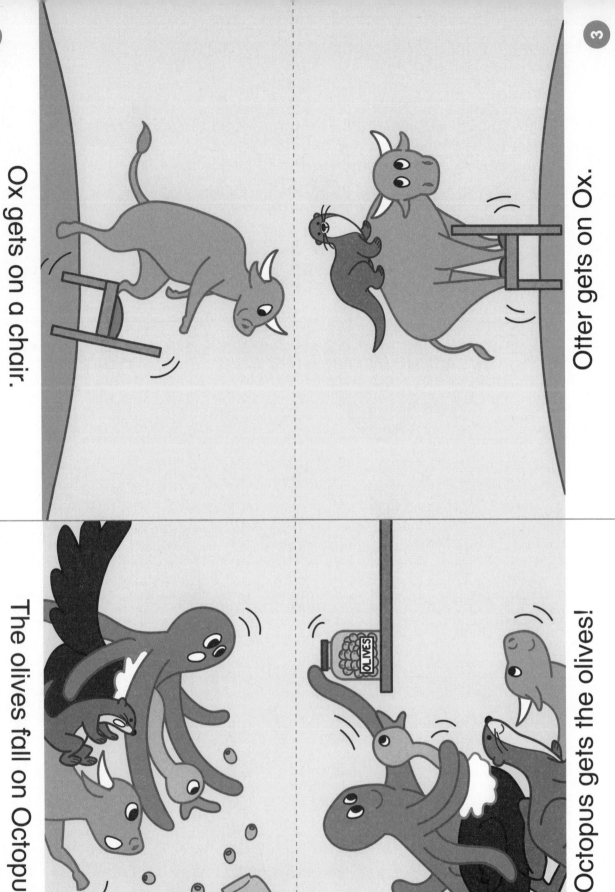

Ox gets on a chair.

Otter gets on Ox.

The olives fall on Octopus.

Octopus gets the olives!

Draw lines to connect the matching uppercase and lowercase letters. The first one has been done for you.

O   n

N   o

m   M

m   O

N   M

o   n

N   m

o   n

M   O

n   N

M   o

O   m

Say the name of each picture.
Write the letter that makes the beginning sound.

_____

- - - - -

_____

_____

- - - - -

_____

_____

- - - - -

_____

_____

- - - - -

_____

_____

- - - - -

_____

_____

- - - - -

_____

Draw a line to connect the pictures that rhyme.
The first one has been done for you.

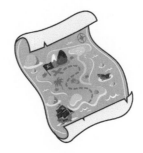

Say the name of each picture. Color the pairs that rhyme.

Write the missing letter in each box. Use words from the Word List.

Word List
with   his   in   they

wi☐h   hi☐   th☐y   i☐

h☐s   ☐ith   ☐n   t☐ey

Use the words from above to complete the sentences.

We are _____ school.

Tom brought _____ rocket.

I play _____ the planets.

Can _____ glow?

Color the picture. Use the Color Key.

Color Key

his   they   in   with

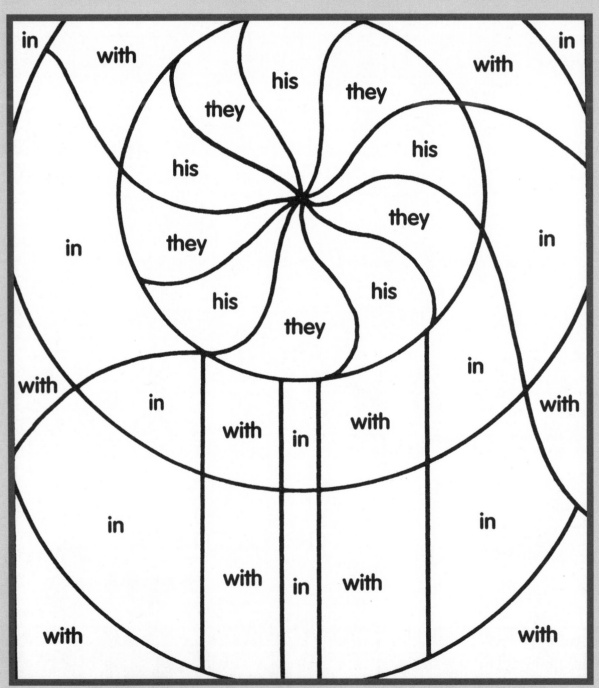

Find and circle seven things that begin with the **p** sound.
The first one has been done for you.

Trace and write **P** and **p**.

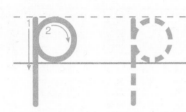

Say the name of each picture. Color it if it begins with the **p** sound. Then, write **p** below the pictures you colored.

Cut out each picture.
If it begins with the **p** sound,
paste it on the pirate ship.

Parrot brings pancakes.

The Picnic

Penguin brings peaches.

Time for a picnic!

Panda brings pizza.

Penguin brings pie.

Porcupine brings popcorn.

Pelican brings pears.

Find and circle seven things that begin with the **q** sound.
The first one has been done for you.

Trace and write **Q** and **q**.

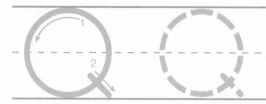

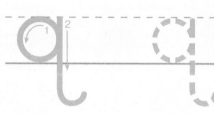

Say the name of each picture.
Write **q** below the picture if it begins with the **q** sound.

Cut out each picture.
If it begins with the **q** sound, paste it on the quilt.

"Quick!" said the man.

Quack! Quiet! Quick!

"Quack!" said the duckling.

"Quack!" "Quiet!" "Quick!"

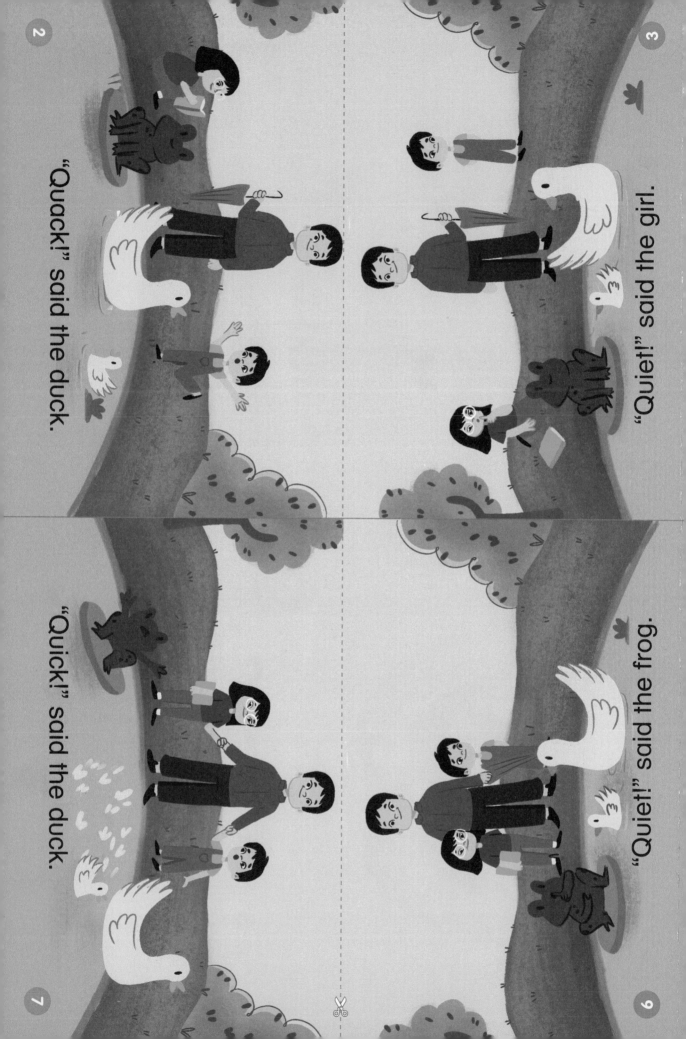

"Quack!" said the duck.

"Quiet!" said the girl.

"Quick!" said the duck.

"Quiet!" said the frog.

2

3

7

6

Find and circle seven things that begin with the **r** sound.
The first one has been done for you.

Trace and write **R** and **r**.

Say the name of each picture. Color it if it begins with the **r** sound. Then, write **r** below the pictures you colored.

Cut out each picture.
If it begins with the **r** sound, paste it under the rain cloud.

I read about roads.

I Read

I read about rivers.

I read about _____ .

I read about

2

I read about rocks.

I read about robots.

I read about rockets.

I read about rabbits.

3

6

2

7

Draw lines to connect the matching uppercase and lowercase letters. The first one has been done for you.

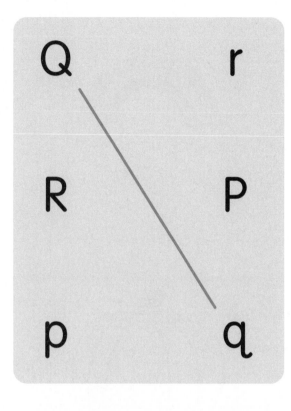

Q	r
R	P
p	q

r	p
q	Q
P	R

R	Q
q	P
p	r

P	r
R	p
q	Q

Say the name of each picture.
Write the letter that makes the beginning sound.

_____

- - - - - - - - - - - - -

_____

_____

- - - - - - - - - - - - -

_____

_____

- - - - - - - - - - - - -

_____

_____

- - - - - - - - - - - - -

_____

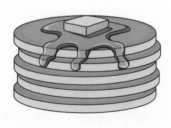

_____

- - - - - - - - - - - - -

_____

_____

- - - - - - - - - - - - -

_____

Draw a line to connect the pictures that rhyme.
The first one has been done for you.

Say the name of each picture. Color the pairs that rhyme.

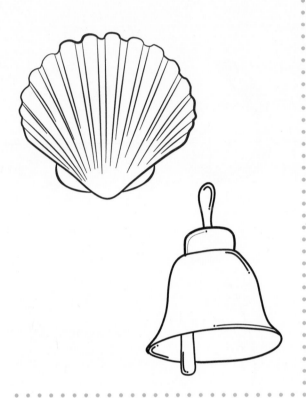

Find and circle seven things that begin with the **s** sound.
The first one has been done for you.

Trace and write **S** and **s**.

Say the name of each picture.
Write **s** below the picture if it begins with the **s** sound.

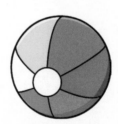

Cut out each picture.
If it begins with the **s** sound, paste it next to the soup.

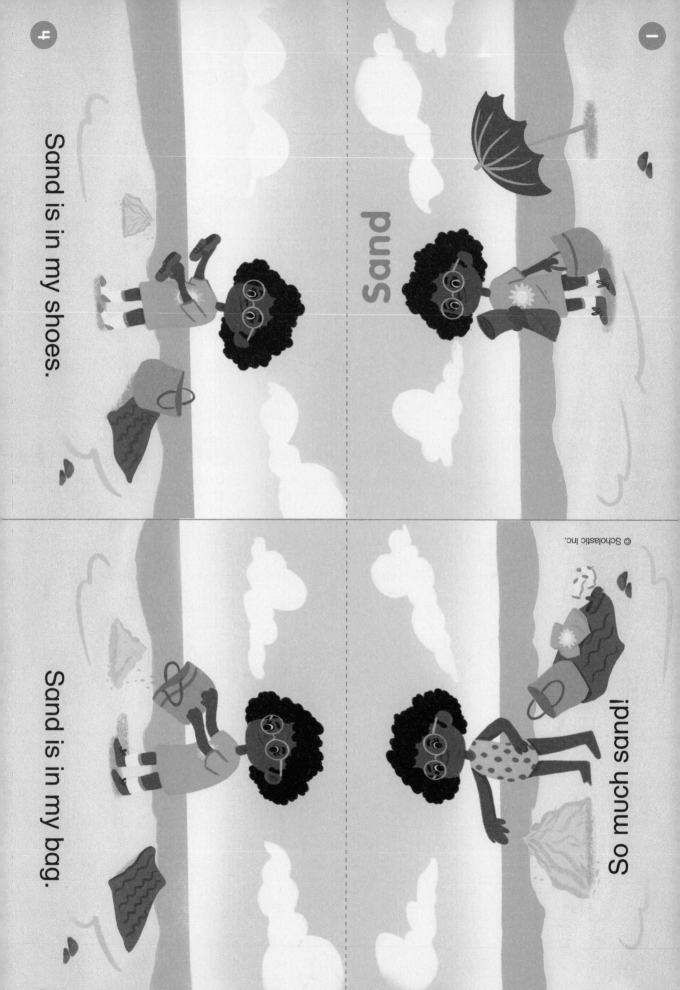

Sand is in my shoes.

Sand

Sand is in my bag.

So much sand!

Sand is in my hat.

Sand is in my towel.

Sand is in my shirt.

Sand is in my socks.

Find and circle seven things that begin with the **t** sound.
The first one has been done for you.

Trace and write **T** and **t**.

Say the name of each picture. Color it if it begins with the **t** sound. Then, write **t** below the pictures you colored.

Cut out each animal.
If it begins with the **t** sound, paste it on the train.

Tails

1

What has a tail?

4

A toucan has a tail.

5

A _____ has a tail, too.

8

2

What has a tail?

3

A tiger has a tail.

7

A turtle has a tail.

6

What has a tail?

Find and circle five things that begin with the **u** sound.
The first one has been done for you.

© Scholastic Inc.

Trace and write **U** and **u**.

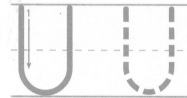

Say the name of each picture.
Write **u** below the picture if it begins with the **u** sound.

Cut out each picture.
If it begins with the **u** sound, paste it under the umbrella.

Up and Under

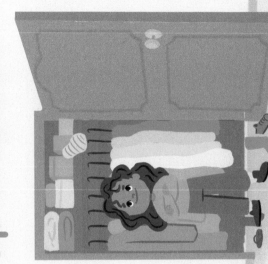

Look in.

Look under.

Pam found the umbrella!

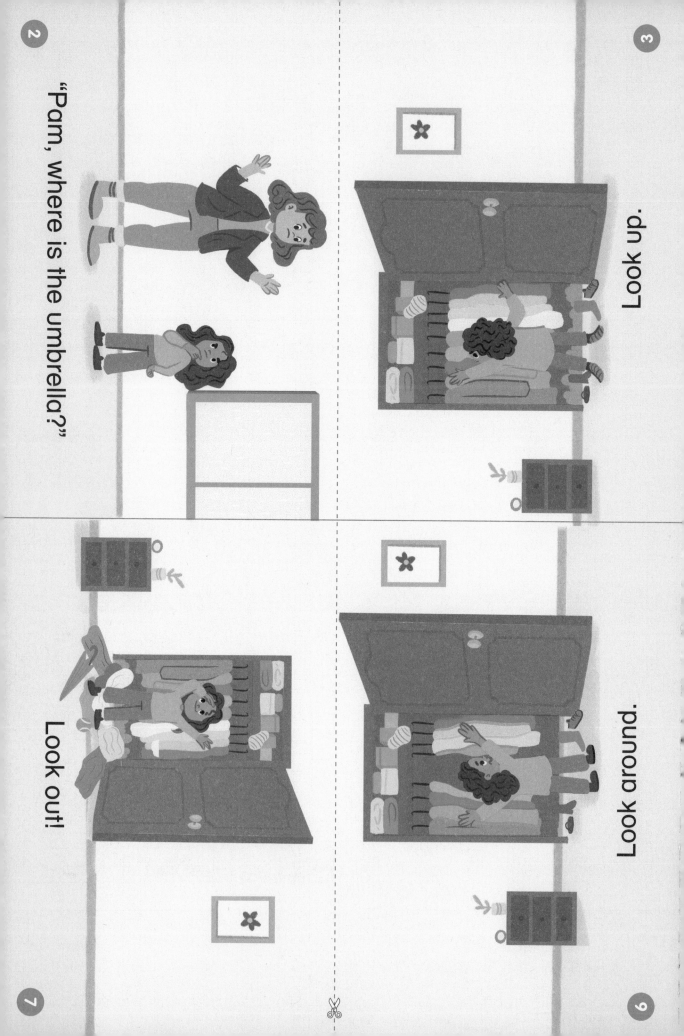

"Pam, where is the umbrella?"

3

Look up.

Look around.

Look out!

Find and circle seven things that begin with the **v** sound.
The first one has been done for you.

Trace and write **V** and **v**.

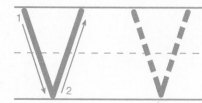

Say the name of each picture. Color it if it begins with the **v** sound. Then, write **v** below the pictures you colored.

Cut out each picture.
If it begins with the **v** sound,
paste it on the vase.

Dogs go to the vet.

To the Vet

Rabbits go to the vet.

Pets go to the vet.

4

1

5

8

Who goes to the vet?

Cats go to the vet.

Birds go to the vet.

Hamsters go to the vet.

Draw lines to connect the matching uppercase and lowercase letters. The first one has been done for you.

S	T	U	v
t	s	S	s
U	v	V	U
V	u	T	t

V	v	t	V
S	t	v	s
u	S	U	T
T	U	S	u

Say the name of each picture.
Write the letter that makes the beginning sound.

_ _ _ _ _ _ _ _

_ _ _ _ _ _ _ _

_ _ _ _ _ _ _ _

_ _ _ _ _ _ _ _

_ _ _ _ _ _ _ _

_ _ _ _ _ _ _ _

_ _ _ _ _ _ _ _

_ _ _ _ _ _ _ _

Draw a line to connect the pictures that rhyme.
The first one has been done for you.

Say the name of each picture. Color the pairs that rhyme.

Find and circle seven things that begin with the **w** sound.
The first one has been done for you.

Trace and write **W** and **w**.

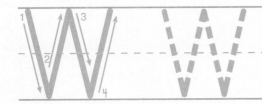

Say the name of each picture. Color it if it begins with the **w** sound. Then, write **w** below the pictures you colored.

© Scholastic Inc.

Cut out each picture.
If it begins with the **w** sound, paste it in the window.

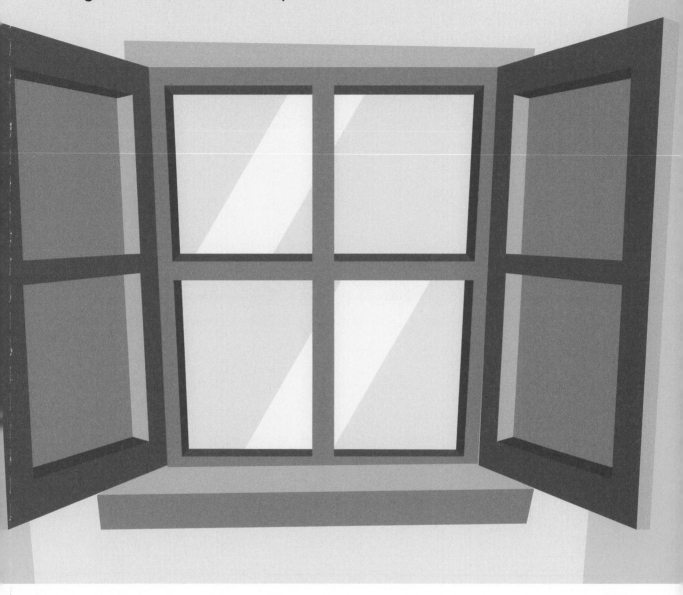

Outside my window is a worm.

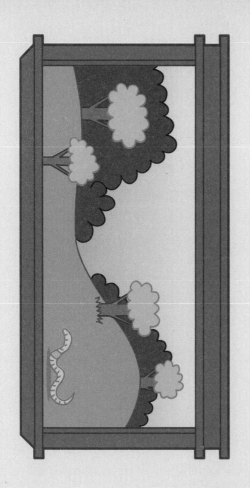

Outside My Window

Outside my window is a _____.

Outside my window is a windmill.

What is outside my window?

Outside my window is a waterfall.

What is outside your window?

Outside my window is a wagon.

Find and circle five things that end with the **x** sound.
The first one has been done for you.

Trace and write **X** and **x**.

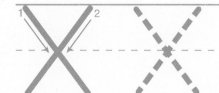

Say the name of each picture.
Write **x** below the picture if it ends with the **x** sound.

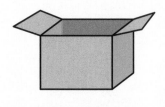

Cut out each picture.
If it ends with the **x** sound, paste it in the box.

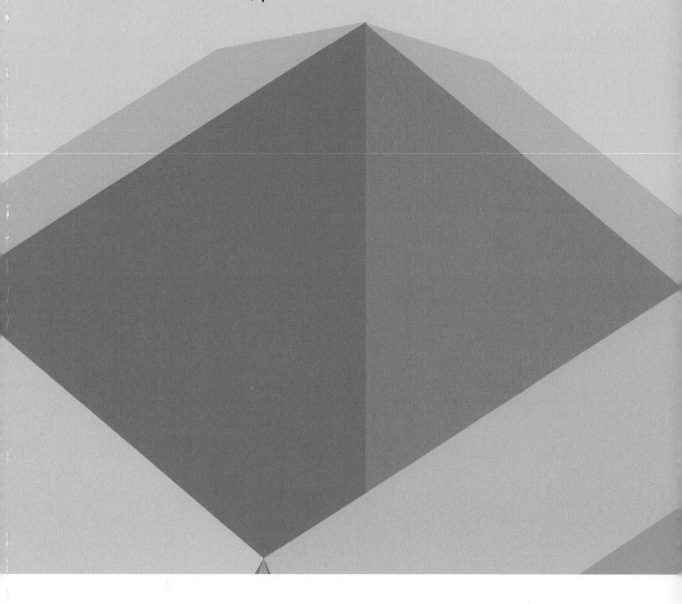

Can a fox fix it?

Fix It

Can a dog fix it?

I can fix it!

Who can fix it?

Can an ox fix it?

Who can fix it?

Can a cat fix it?

Find and circle six things that begin with the **y** sound.
The first one has been done for you.

Trace and write **Y** and **y**.

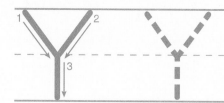

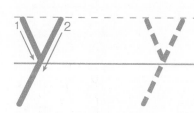

Say the name of each picture. Color it if it begins with the **y** sound. Then, write **y** below the pictures you colored.

Cut out each picture.
If it begins with the **y** sound, paste it on the yo-yo.

4

I see a yellow car.

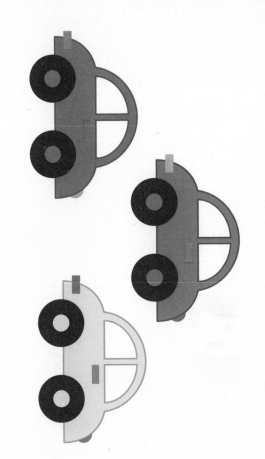

1

Yellow

5

I see a yellow boat.

8

I see a yellow kite.

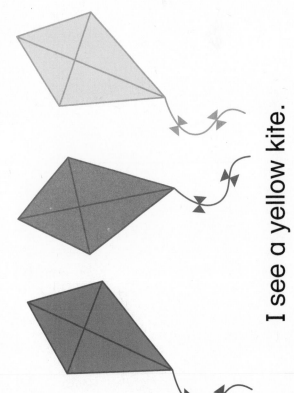

I see a yellow yo-yo.

I see a yellow ball.

I see a yellow shirt.

I see a yellow block.

Find and circle five things that begin with the **z** sound.
The first one has been done for you.

Trace and write **Z** and **z**.

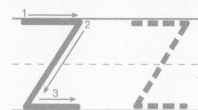

Say the name of each picture. Color it if it begins with the **z** sound. Then, write **z** below the pictures you colored.

Cut out each picture.
If it begins with the **z** sound, paste it at the end of a zigzag.

It can zig-zag.

Zig Zag Zoom

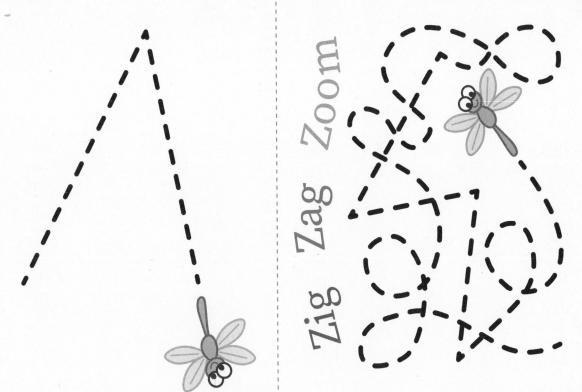

It can zoom.

It can zig, zag, zig-zag, zoom, zip, and zap.

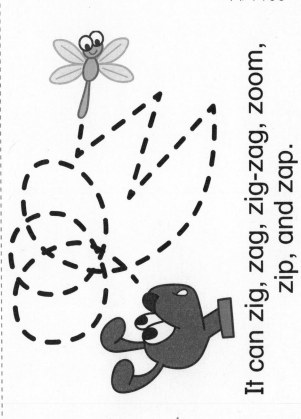

It can zig.

It can zag.

It can zap.

It can zip.

Draw lines to connect the matching uppercase and lowercase letters. The first one has been done for you.

W		Z
Z		W
X		Y
y		x

X		Y
y		x
Z		W
w		z

Y		x
W		z
X		y
Z		W

X		Z
y		W
z		Y
W		x

© Scholastic Inc.

Say the name of each picture.
Write the letter that makes the beginning sound.

_____

- - - - - - - -

_____

_____

- - - - - - - -

_____

_____

- - - - - - - -

_____

_____

- - - - - - - -

_____

_____

- - - - - - - -

_____

_____

- - - - - - - -

_____

Listen to the poem as your parent or caregiver reads it aloud.

> Some days I wear a smile
> Stretched wide like a crocodile.
>
> Some days I wear a frown
> Hung heavy like a crown.
>
> Some days I shine like the sun.
> I skip and hop and run.
>
> Some days I let out a laugh
> That stretches to the tallest giraffe.

Draw a line to connect the pictures that rhyme. The first one has been done for you.

Say the name of each picture. Color the pairs that rhyme.

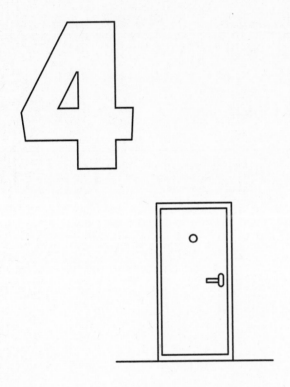

Color the letters in your name.
Then, write your name on the lunch box.

WORD FAMILIES

Once your child has mastered letter sounds, he or she will be ready to conquer word families! Word families are one of the most effective vehicles for developing literacy skills.

Word families are groups of words that share a common ending. For example: *man, van, pan*, and *can* are all part of the **-an** word family. Studying the many common word families boosts a child's ability to read and write words exponentially.

For example, can your little one spell *cat*? Then he or she can spell *mat, rat, hat, bat*, and so much more! When children can recognize these word chunks, their ability to decode and comprehend soars.

Find and circle five things that end in **-at** as in *pat*.
The first one has been done for you.

Write the correct **-at** word under each picture.
Use words from the Word List.

Word List
hat cat bat rat

_____

- - - - - - - - - - - - - - -

_____

_____

- - - - - - - - - - - - - - -

_____

_____

- - - - - - - - - - - - - - -

_____

_____

- - - - - - - - - - - - - - -

_____

Make an -at word family slide!

1. Cut along the dashed lines below.
2. Weave the letter and picture strips through the correct slots.
3. Slide the strips up or down to match words and pictures.

at

That is a bat.

What Is That?

What is that?

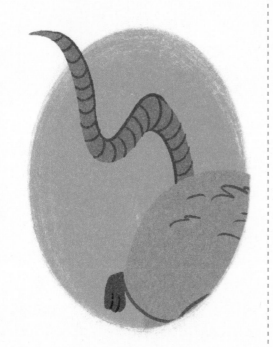

That is Pat.

That is a cat.

What is that?

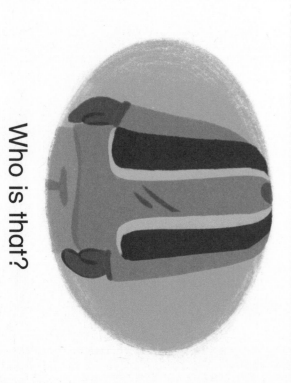

Who is that?

That is a rat.

Find and circle five things that end in **-an** as in *ran*.
The first one has been done for you.

Write the correct **-an** word under each picture.
Use words from the Word List.

Word List
pan   can   van   man

_____

- - - - - - - - - - - -

_____

_____

- - - - - - - - - - - -

_____

_____

- - - - - - - - - - - -

_____

_____

- - - - - - - - - - - -

_____

Make an -an word family slide!

1 Cut along the dashed lines below.

2 Weave the letter and picture strips through the correct slots.

3 Slide the strips up or down to match words and pictures.

an

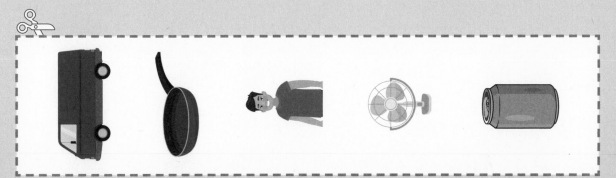

They All Ran

4

The dog ran.

Nan ran.

Mouse hops on the van.
Bye, Mouse!

2

The mouse ran.

3

The cat ran.

6

Dan ran.

7

Mouse makes a plan.

Cut out the cookies. Paste each on the correct jar.

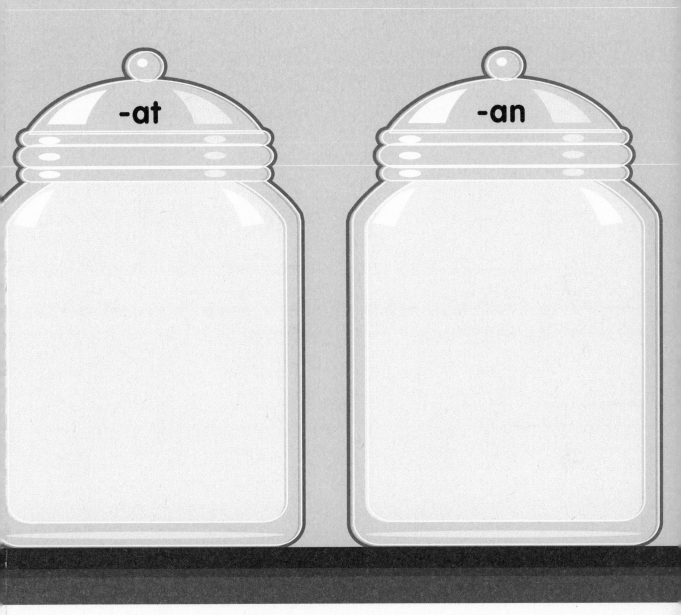

-at

-an

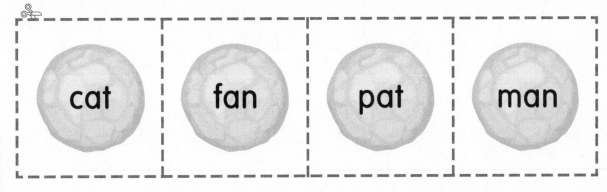

cat fan pat man

Find and circle five things that end in **-ip** as in *hip*.
The first one has been done for you.

Write the correct **-ip** word under each picture.
Use words from the Word List.

Word List
hip   rip   sip   drip

_____

- - - - - - - - - - - - - -

_____

_____

- - - - - - - - - - - - - -

_____

- - - - - - - - - - - - - -

_____

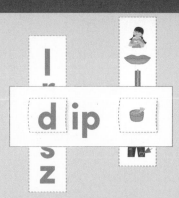

Make an -ip word family slide!

1 Cut along the dashed lines below.

2 Weave the letter and picture strips through the correct slots.

3 Slide the strips up or down to match words and pictures.

ip

l r d s z

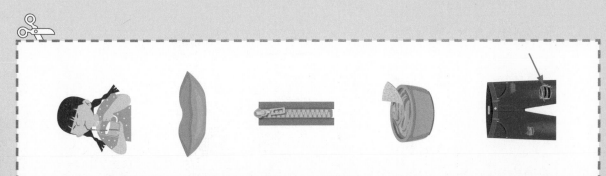

Pip's Ship

Pip sees his pal, Kip.

Pip and Kip eat chips and dip.

What a yummy trip!

2

Pip is on a ship.

3

Pip is going on a trip.

7

Pip and Kip sip and sip.

6

Don't let the dip drip, Pip!

Find and circle five things that end in **-ed** as in *led*.
The first one has been done for you.

Write the correct **-ed** word under each picture.
Use words from the Word List.

Word List
bed   red   Ted   sled

_____

_____

_____

_____

_____

_____

_____

_____

Make an -ed word family slide!

1 Cut along the dashed lines below.

2 Weave the letter and picture strips through the correct slots.

3 Slide the strips up or down to match words and pictures.

Ned sees a red Ted.

Ned Sees Red

Ned sees a red sled.

Ned sees Ed, Fred, and Zed wearing red.

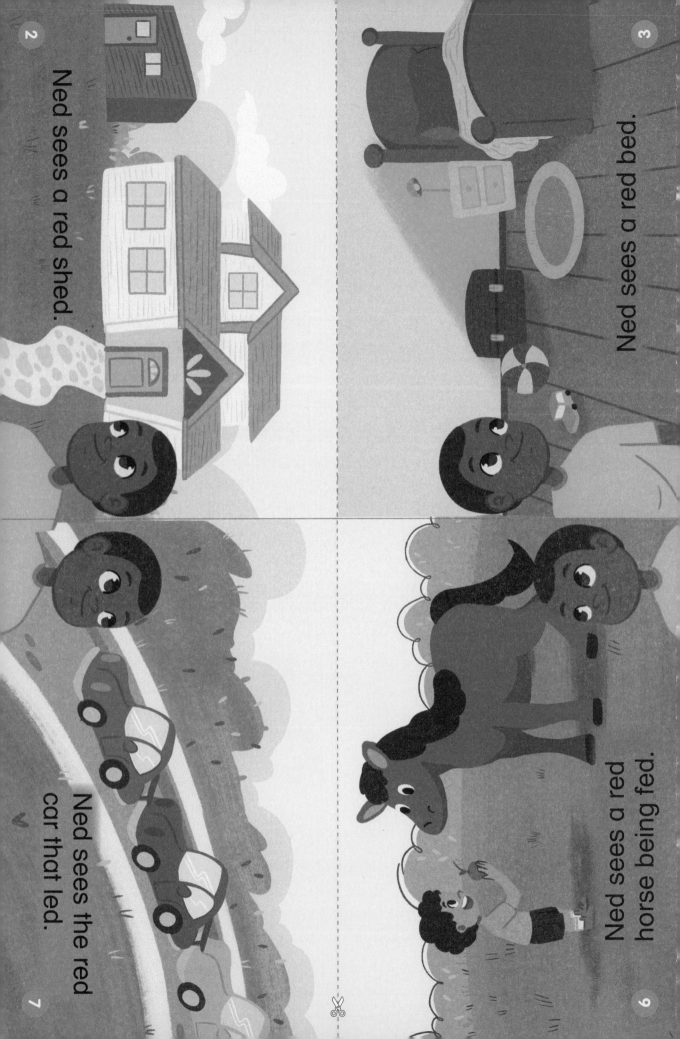

Ned sees a red bed.

Ned sees a red shed.

Ned sees a red
horse being fed.

Ned sees the red
car that led.

Cut out the shells. Paste each below the correct crab.

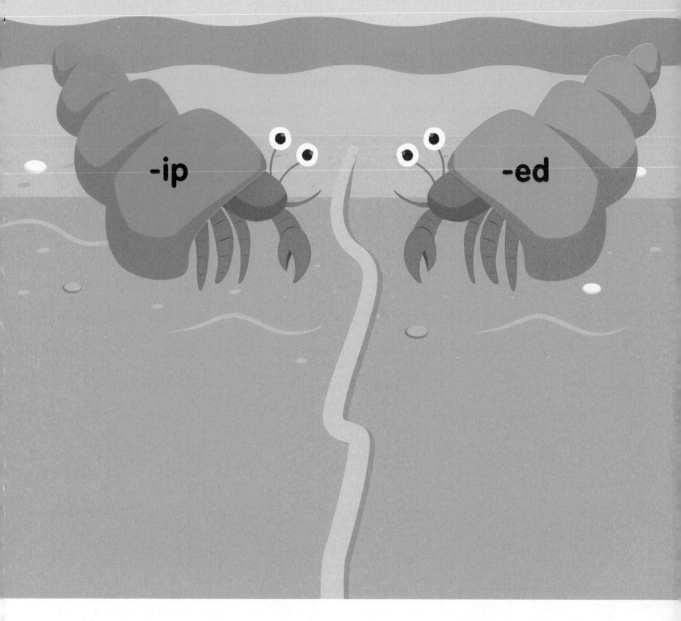

-ip

-ed

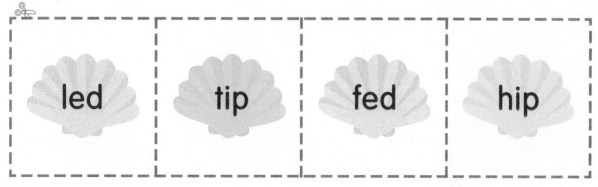

led   tip   fed   hip

Find and circle five things that end in **-en** as in *den*.
The first one has been done for you.

Write the correct **-en** word under each picture.
Use words from the Word List.

Word List
men   hen   pen   ten

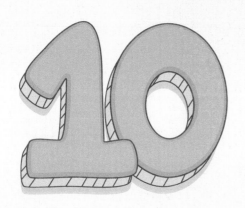

_____

_____

_____

_____

Make an -en word family slide!

1 Cut along the dashed lines below.
2 Weave the letter and picture strips through the correct slots.
3 Slide the strips up or down to match words and pictures.

en

4

I see ten hens.

5

I see ten jets.

1

I SEE TEN

10 10 10 10 10 10 10 10 10 10

8

I see ten _____

I see ten hats.

I see ten men.

I see ten eggs.

I see ten nests.

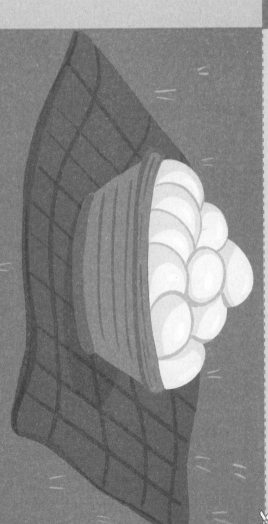

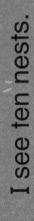

Find and circle five things that end in **-ug** as in *tug*.
The first one has been done for you.

Write the correct **-ug** word under each picture.
Use words from the Word List.

Word List
bug rug jug mug

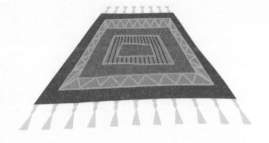

_____

- - - - - - - - - - - -

_____

_____

- - - - - - - - - - - -

_____

_____

- - - - - - - - - - - -

_____

_____

- - - - - - - - - - - -

_____

Make an -ug word family slide!

1. Cut along the dashed lines below.
2. Weave the letter and picture strips through the correct slots.
3. Slide the strips up or down to match words and pictures.

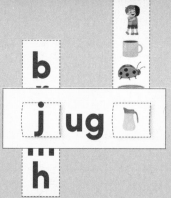

Pug is on a rug.

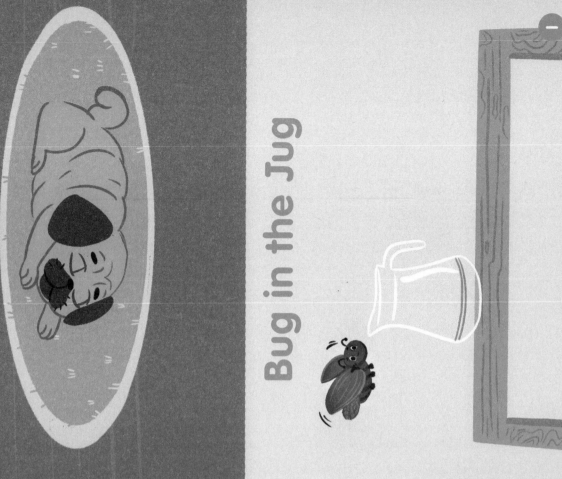

Bug in the Jug

Pug sees Bug in the jug.

Bug gives Pug a mug.

Uh-oh! Bug fell in the jug.

Bug does not feel snug.

Pug and Bug hug.

Pug frees Bug.

Cut out the treats. Paste each on the correct bowl.

-en   -ug

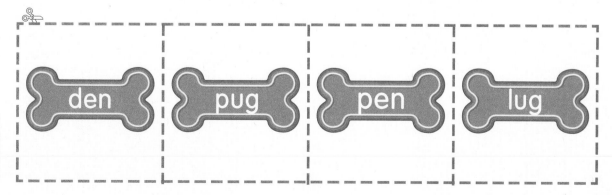

den   pug   pen   lug

Find and circle five things that end in **-op** as in *pop*.
The first one has been done for you.

Candy
SHOP

STOP

OPEN

Write the correct **-op** word under each picture.
Use words from the Word List.

Word List
hop   top   mop   pop

Make an -op word family slide!

1 Cut along the dashed lines below.

2 Weave the letter and picture strips through the correct slots.

3 Slide the strips up or down to match words and pictures.

op

t   dr   m   p   h

4

Rabbit hops on top.

Who Hops on Top?

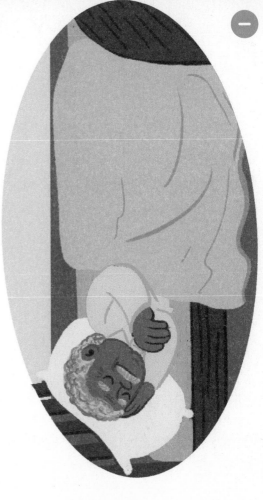

Squirrel hops on top.

They all hop on top! Sleep tight!

Shh! Pop is sleeping.

Kangaroo hops on top.

Cricket hops on top.

Frog hops on top.

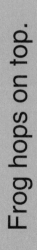

Find and circle four things that end in **-un** as in *fun*.
The first one has been done for you.

Write the correct **-un** word under each picture.
Use words from the Word List.

Word List
fun   sun   bun   run

_____

- - - - - - - - - - - -

_____

_____

- - - - - - - - - - - -

_____

_____

- - - - - - - - - - - -

_____

_____

- - - - - - - - - - - -

_____

Make an -un word family slide!

1 Cut along the dashed lines below.
2 Weave the letter and picture strips through the correct slots.
3 Slide the strips up or down to match words and pictures.

un

It is fun to jump.

Fun!

It is fun to nap in the sun.

A sunny day is full of fun!

It is fun to swim.

It is fun to run.

It is fun to read.

It is fun to play.

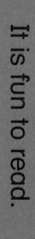

Cut out the fish. Paste each in the correct pond.

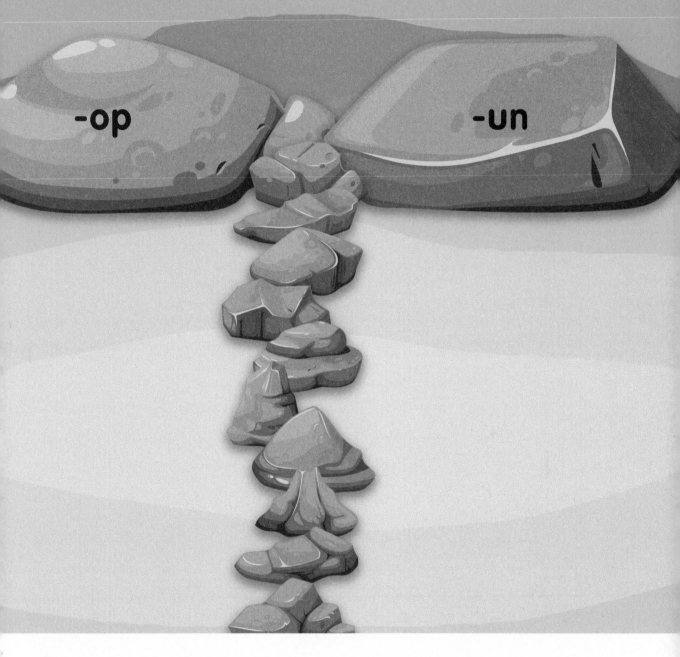

-op

-un

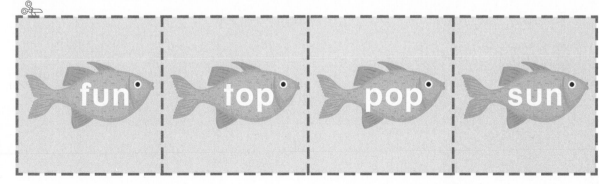

fun

top

pop

sun

Field Day Fun!

Draw your favorite field day game.

8

Can you hop like Ned and Nan?

Can you bat like Mat and Mip?

Can you tug like Pat and Pip?

Can you pop balloons like Jun and Jen?

Can you run like Kip and Ken?

Can you sled like Dug and Dan?

FLASH CARDS

Flash cards are a fun and playful tool to reinforce learning. They allow learners of all ages to interact with information in a way that makes it easier to retain, which helps enhance and encourage recall. Children can quickly learn new words, facts, or concepts via flash cards. When used regularly, flash cards create stronger connections that improve learning.

The pages that follow include three sets of flash cards:

Alphabet Flash Cards   303–308
Word Family Flash Cards   309–310
Sight Word Flash Cards   **311–314**

To use the flash cards, remove pages 303–318 along the perforations. Then carefully cut apart the flash cards. To keep the cards tidy, store them in a plastic zip-close bag or shoebox. Use the blank flash cards to extend learning—write new sight words, word families, or names of family and friends.

Making and Using the Flash Cards

Here are some ways to use the flash cards.

ALPHABET FLASH CARDS

Cut apart the cards on pages 303–308. Show your child the picture and ask what sound he or she hears at the beginning. Then, brainstorm more words that begin with that letter.

WORD FAMILY FLASH CARDS

Cut apart the cards on pages 309–310. Show your child the picture and ask what word family he or she hears at the end. Then, turn the card over and ask your child to say other words that make the same ending sound.

SIGHT WORD FLASH CARDS

Cut apart the cards on pages 311–314. Hold up a card and ask your child to read it. Then, turn the card over to read the word on the other side.

FILL-IN-THE-BLANKS

Continue the learning! There are blank cards included in each group. Use these blank cards to practice new word families and additional sight words.

FUN FLASH CARD ACVITIVTIES

1. **GO FISH:** Place some flash cards in a bag. Invite your child to draw a card and read it aloud. If the card is read correctly, he or she keeps it. When 10 cards are collected, your child wins.

2. **SEEK-AND-READ:** Place 10 flash cards around a room and set a timer for two minutes. Can your child find and read all 10 cards before the timer goes off?

3. **SILLY SENTENCES:** Ask your child to pick three flash cards. Can he or she make a sentence that includes all three words?

Aa	Ff
Bb	Gg
Cc	Hh
Dd	Ii
Ee	Jj

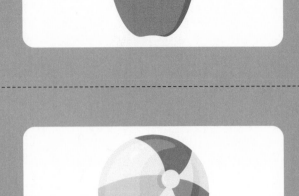

Kk	Pp
Ll	Qq
Mm	Rr
Nn	Ss
Oo	Tt

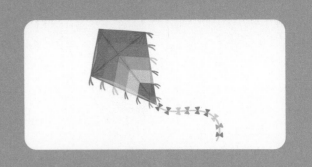

Uu

Xx

Vv

Yy

Ww

Zz

-ip	-at
-en	-an
-ug	-ed
-op	-un

 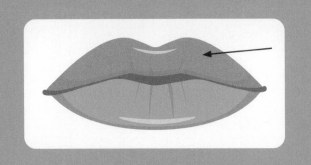

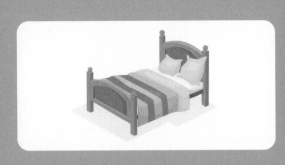 

the	is
of	am
can	you
and	that
to	it

he	as
was	with
for	his
on	they
are	in

at	she
be	had
this	by
have	but
from	not

we

all

Answer Key

For pages not shown, please check your child's work.

Page 32

Page 33

Page 35

Page 41

Page 47

Page 55
Rhymes: cat → hat,
dog → frog; tree → bee,
car → star; map → nap,
rug → bug; book → cook,
fox → box

Page 56
Rhymes: bat → rat;
mug → hug; key → three

Page 59

Page 65

Page 71

Page 79
Rhymes: chair → hair,
doll → ball; swing → ring,
hook → book; wheel →
seal, fan → van; mice →

dice, dive → hive

Page 80
Rhymes: bear → pear; goat → coat; goose → moose

Page 83

Page 89

Page 95

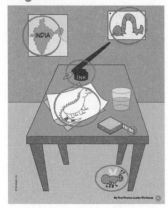

Page 103
Rhymes: net → vet, pin → fin; sun → run, cake → rake; duck → truck,

eye → pie; clock → sock, snail → tail

Page 104
Rhymes: man → pan; lock → rock; kitten → mitten

Page 107

Page 113

Page 119

Page 127
Rhymes: ring → swing; pie → fly; top → mop; stone → bone

Page 128
Rhymes: ox → box; lamp → stamp; nurse → purse

Page 131

Page 137

Page 143

Page 151
Rhymes: mouse → house, wag → bag; pool → stool, bone → cone; cheese → bees, sled → bed; map → cap, shoe → two

Page 152
Rhymes: bread → bed; eight → gate; frog → dog

Page 155

Page 161

Page 167

Page 175
Rhymes: stop → hop; glue → blue; carrot → parrot; tail → sail; light → knight; pants → ants; chick → stick; swing → king

Page 176
Rhymes: shell → bell; dragon → wagon; snake → cake

Page 179

Page 185

Page 191

Page 197

Page 205
Rhymes: eel → seal; bee → key; dog → log; clam → lamb; pool → school; money → honey; ten → hen; moon → spoon

Page 206
Rhymes: fox → socks; bat → cat; bear → chair

Page 209

Page 215

Page 241

Page 269

Page 221

Page 247

Page 275

Page 227

Page 255

Page 283

Page 235
Rhymes: sun → run;
smile → crocodile;
frown → crown;
giraffe → laugh

Page 236
Rhymes: four → door;
goat → boat; plane → train

Page 261

Page 289

Great work!

Fantastic!

Good job!

Excellent!

Congratulations!

is a Phonics Superstar!

Hip, Hip, Hooray!

SCHOLASTIC